SHACKLED YET FREE

DENNIS A. MCINTYRE

Bennett Media and Marketing
1603 Capitol Ave., Suite 310 A233
Cheyenne, WY 82001
www.thebennettmediaandmarketing.com
Phone: 1-307-202-9292

ISBN: 978-1-957114-08-8 (Paperback)
ISBN: 978-1-957114-09-5 (eBook)

Library of Congress Control Number: 2022902306

Printed in the United States of America

Any people depicted in stock imagery provided by Shutterstock are models, and such images are being used for illustrative purposes only.

Certain stock imagery © Shutterstock. This book is printed on acid-free paper.

Because of the dynamic nature of the Internet, any web addresses or links contained in this book may have changed since publication and may no longer be valid. The views expressed in this work are solely those of the author and do not necessarily reflect the views of the publisher, and the publisher hereby disclaims any responsibility for them.

About the Author

DENNIS A. MCINTYRE is a native of Rochester, NY, and served as an electrical engineer and a technical writer for over 40 years before retiring. Since retirement, Dennis has focused his efforts on his personal writing, publishing his first book, an autobiographical work entitled *Legacy of Love*, in 2008 through Tate Publishing. Dennis currently resides in Dacula, GA, and attends Anchor Church, in Grayson, GA. He enjoys using his gifts of encouraging and writing for the glory of God's kingdom. His main goal for writing involves drawing people into closer relationships with the Lord and one another.

Contents

Legal Proceedings

The courthouse was unusually quiet that March afternoon. Although the orange blossoms were in full bloom, there was little evidence of pollen on the steps or inside the atrium area. The sunlight made the marble walls glisten, and the floors appeared clean enough to eat on. If cleanliness was truly next to godliness, then the court system appeared with a heavenly glow. I felt as though I should remove my shoes.

I was often called in to provide background and character information for clients called for judicial reviews or hearings. My job as a parole officer kept a watchful eye on those under my charge. I knew Jake for over twenty years. His past was filled with misdemeanors, drugs, alcohol, larceny, and rebellion against authority. Yet, as I watched him interact with his wife and children in the corner of the large waiting area outside the courtroom, I could see a man at peace. His face was clean-shaven, unlike the rough exterior that I have been used to. He was wearing a suit, which was in sharp contrast to the much worn jeans and uncollared shirt worn in his plumbing trade. Jake could pass himself off as a minister today. It was a startling change to be sure from the man I knew, one that brought a warm smile to my face.

Jake was a man who welcomed a brawl. The ball and chain tattoo on his ankle was a constant reminder of his incarceration in a Federal prison for grand theft nearly fifteen years ago. His physical appearance included multiple battle scars. Although his hair was beginning to recede, it was thick and full without gray. I could only imagine that if his head was shaved, we might witness a roadmap of additional battle wounds. Then again, we might read it as a treasure map with "X" marking the spot where Jake became a changed man. I feel privileged to have seen the transformation.

As I watched Jake interact with his children, I was reminded about the background information that I accumulated as his parole officer. Some of it came from Jake himself during long one-on-one sessions with him as a teenager. He was now in his mid thirties. Parents, relatives, neighbors, teachers, and other acquaintances helped to fill in the blanks. His childhood was filled with setbacks. Although he was born in a small rural town in Indiana, circumstances did not create the euphoric view of Mayberry, USA.

Jake's earliest recollection of his childhood was when he was about four years old. He remembers his dad leaving one day and never coming back. Initially, it was not unusual. His father would leave before Jake would get out of bed to go to work. Jake was too young to remember what his dad did for a living. His mother was pregnant at the time and did not work. Jake's father was rarely home with a busy work schedule. Because of that, there was little interaction between Jake and his dad. On the day his father left, mom sat Jake down on the bed and began a conversation that made little sense at the time.

> She began by saying, *"Jake, your daddy does not live here anymore."*
> *"What do you mean mommy?"*
> *"Daddy does not love your mommy anymore."*
> *"Mommy, he could sleep in my room."*
> *"Daddy has found someone else to live with, son."* His mother tried to console Jake without causing further distress.
> *"But mommy, doesn't daddy love me anymore?"*

Jake's mother held back the tears and tried fervently to assure her son that his father still loved him. The weeks, months, and years that followed only served to convince Jake otherwise. The concept of love for Jake was distorted early in his life. What is love? How is it measured? Love for Jake was not a verb, which implies action. His father was there one moment and gone the next. Watching other boys playing catch with their dads would certainly have been a new experience for Jake, as spending time alone with his father was limited to some form of chastisement. The words, "Doesn't daddy love me anymore?" penetrated his mom's heart with deep conviction. Perhaps, she wondered if the father of her child had ever loved their son. In that moment of reflection, her tears streamed down her face and one four-year old boy watched with a sense of fear that he might lose a mother as well. Dad's leaving had a profound and lasting effect on Jake throughout his entire life.

A father's love is a very important commodity, especially during the first five years of a boy's life. Jake had a father but was void of any meaningful relationship. He did not witness any emotional connection with his parents. He understood scolding as the only form of love shown by his father. Mom provided a milder form of council. Any concept of love would have been watered down. Jake was four years old physically, but emotionally still in infancy. We may grow physically and take on all the attributes of manhood, but stymied emotional growth will rear its ugly head in adulthood. That appeared to be the case for Jake. The emotions he learned were bitterness and hate. The only form of love he would learn during his impressionable early years came from those he hung with. Many of those also came from broken homes.

His father did not leave mom for another woman. He left for a new life with a man. In the seventies this relationship was not openly discussed and carried with it the scar of abandonment. Just like that, dad was out of Jake's life for good. Mom had to find work and a new place to live. Jake was now the man of the house. The loss of a father in Jake's life may not have brought on outward indicators in Jake's demeanor, but it had a profound impact in his life. His fatherless years had few boundaries. In short, Jake became a spoiled brat. If an occasional spanking was the only love Jake ever received from his dad, then even that was gone.

Jake was five when his sister was born. Now they were a family of three. Jake was the big brother, but mom was busy trying to keep food on the table and a roof over their heads. Dad left suddenly and completely. There was no alimony or child support money to help offset expenses. Jake was in a survival mode at an early age. Today, he is facing a new form of survival. The custody hearing is moments away, and the welfare of his much-loved teenage daughters hangs in the balance. Looking across the foyer, I can see lines of worry on his face. His third wife of eight years is gently caressing him as if to say that everything will be all right. This quick-tempered man looks beaten. Yet, I sense an amazing calmness in his spirit, as if everything will be all right.

Jake's adopted children are playfully seeking his attention. They are from his wife's first marriage, which ended in a brutal divorce. Her ex-husband left for another woman and wanted nothing to do with his children. Jake was the father they never had, and it showed. The playful teasing and genuine laughter would warm the hearts of anyone near them. Jake was not the same man I knew during his years of incarceration and probation. He understands what it means to be loved and how to love in return. The burning anger that I saw within Jake has been replaced with a calm serenity. He has learned fatherhood from his relationship with his heavenly father, and it shows.

The waiting area is unusually quiet this day. It is nearly four in the afternoon. The courtroom activity this morning was frenzy. Most of the cases were over or dismissed, but a few remained in session. We've been waiting for over an hour, which was expected. Court cases were not like doctor visits, where some degree of measurable timeframe was associated with each procedure. The courts did the best they could to schedule cases, and Jake's was considered to be one that could be handled late in the day. The feeling, however, was that it may be further delayed to another date if the present case is not concluded soon. The agony of waiting and the uncertainty of the outcome may be taking its toll on Jake.

The wait is also causing anxious moments for me. My testimony may not help Jake's cause. I can only anticipate the questions that will be asked of me. If this was a jury trial, then there might be those who see past the dark side of this man. But, this custody case goes before a judge and the ex-wife is a police officer. Her life may appear saintly in comparison. Over the last eight years I have witnessed a changed man. I can only hope that the judge bases his or her decisions on Jake's character as of today, for the one who answered to me during his probation years was suspect at best.

Waiting to be called into the courtroom has created some anxiety for me, but Jake appears so calm. Lisa, his wife, is gently tapping her husband on his shoulder as if to say that whatever happens, everything will be okay. It seems to be working. This was not the Jake I knew during his parole years. The fire inside the man I knew was no longer burning with rage.

He had found peace. Joy is a new fruit, which is obvious as he wrestles gently with his nine-year-old son. I smiled, warmly, as I was blessed by the transformation from the man of turmoil to the man of peace.

For years I have tried to give council to Jake on a regular basis, and now wish that I could receive it from him. He has found his answers to the burning questions about what love is. He has become the kind of father that he could only wish that he had while growing up. He acts with such gentleness towards his family. His rough looking exterior might cause a stranger to turn away, yet I see those passing by taking the time to say hello and offer casual conversation. There is something very appealing about Jake today. The acquaintances, who knew him as I did, had a totally different reaction, beginning with fear. Jake was the man they wanted on their side in an alley brawl. The transformation is amazing and fills this parole officer's heart with great satisfaction, yet I take no credit for it. My name is Officer Patterson.

This is Jake's story. I am excited to share it, as he has had a huge impact on my life. Let me take you back to his early years as he described them to me. God got a hold of a troubled boy and worked a miracle.

THE STEP DAD

Jake was six years old when a new man came into his life. After his father left, Jake and his mom moved to a small apartment upstairs in a Cape Cod home. Another family rented the lower two-bedroom apartment. The roof was steep, leaving a narrow center area where people can walk without ducking their heads, except for a couple of dormer areas with windows to the front yard. The outside walls were four-foot high, but more than adequate for Jake to freely run around. Furniture was pretty sparse, so the apartment appeared larger inside than it really was. When Jake's sister was born, the walls may have felt like they were closing in, but it was now home.

The Randolph's, Joan, Bob and their son Jimmy were living in the downstairs apartment. The boys became friends almost immediately, as did the mothers. Jake's mother openly shared her life story with Joan. The discussion around locating someone to watch her children so she could earn a living was quickly resolved. Joan offered to provide a safe haven for Jake and his sister, while mom worked as a waitress a few blocks away. Jimmy was about Jake's age and Joan adored children, so the idea seemed to be a natural fit. Joan also had a loving spirit and saw the opportunity to help a family in need.

Jake experienced a new form of love and witnessed family life different from anything he had seen or felt before. Her husband, Bob, also loved children and eagerly supported his wife as a caregiver. Often, he would come home and help before Jake's mom finished work. This may well have been an unusual scene for Jake as his father was almost never home before he went to bed. One can only wonder if this caring family was placed in Jake's life for that exact purpose. Somehow, Jake's mom had secured a place to stay without an income, directly above a family that offered the support she needed to move on with her life.

The home had a center entrance and twelve steps rose sharply upward to the apartment. These steps were well worn and not very attractive. Jake could always tell when company was coming as each step had a familiar creaking sound. The house also had a full basement, where the owner offered storage space for the extra non-essential living items. A box of used paint cans was among the stored items.

The basement became a welcomed escape from the small apartment for Jake and the boy living downstairs. War games were often played and Jake considered opening the small can of bright red paint to use as blood. The idea may have held much higher consequences, however, when mom found paint-smeared clothes. The box of partially used paint cans was still an attraction. The idea of creating a masterpiece may not have been on Jake's mind, but he thought about those ugly steps leading upstairs to the apartment. *"A good coat of paint is just the right thing,"* Jake thought. Inside the box were several old paintbrushes as well. Jake decided to tackle the task of painting the steps. *"Painting each step a different color should do the trick."* His intentions may have been honorable, but after mom came home that evening, the pride on Jake's face was immediately wiped away. The conversation, as Jake told me, went something like this:

"J.D. come down here right now."

Whenever his mother shouted his initials, Jake knew it was important.

> *"Are you surprised, mom?"*
> *"Who painted these steps?"* (Each step was painted a different color and the quality was more like a five year old trying to color inside the lines.)
> *"I did, mom. Doesn't it look great?"*
> *"Who told you to paint the steps?"*
> *"You said that they needed paintin, mama. I was playing in the basement and found the old paint cans."*

By this time Jake started down the stairs towards his mother. His shirt was spackled with the different colors along with his new pants. The multi-colored staircase may have looked like a work of art to Jake, but not to his mother.

> *"Mr. Benson (the landlord) is going to have a fit. Your clothes*
> *are ruined, and I can't afford to buy new ones."*
> *" I thought you would be happy, mommy."*
> *"You are grounded for a week young man."*
> *"But mama …"*
> *"Don't you sass me or you will get your bottom sore as well.*
> *A good spanking might serve you well anyway."*

Jake never forgot the event. Somehow, it had etched a permanent spot in his memory as a defining moment in his life. When Jake shared that story with me years later, I could see resentment in his face. It may have been the first time that he tried to do something nice for his mother, and it exploded in his face. It would help shape his character and esteem for a long time. Perhaps, the only way it would have been more catastrophic is if his father witnessed the stairway. His father's reaction would have affected much more than Jake's character.

Mom would have gentlemen callers on a regular basis come to their apartment. Each time, Jake would be sent to his room prior to their arrival. Jake didn't mind, however, because he had a small television and plenty of snack food, which he confiscated from the pantry in anticipation. Besides, he didn't really care to meet any man who might take over as his father. Memories of his dad walking out were still quite vivid, and despite the moments of rebuke from his mom, Jake was enjoying his spoiled life.

Joe was an army sergeant. He would come over quite regularly, so Jake's small bedroom became his sanctuary. Jake often heard Joe's deep strong voice through the bedroom walls and compensated by turning the television volume up. This move created an escalating series of events, leading to undesired results.

> *"Turn that TV down, Jake."*
> *"I will when you stop talking so loud out there."*
> *"Don't talk to your mom like that Jake,"* Joe added.
> *"I can talk to my mama anyway I want. You're not my dad."*

> *"You need to learn respect young man, and I am just the one to teach you."*

Jake turned the television volume up to the maximum as if to shut out the sound of Joe's voice. A brief moment of silence and then the bedroom door flew open. Joe stormed in as if he was about to reprimand one of his platoon men for insurrection. Without hesitation, Jake received the wrath of Joe's anger. Mom watched with approval.

> *"I am glad you are here to see what I have to deal with on a daily basis, Joe."*
>
> *"Jake needs structure in his life. The military can break his spirit for sure."*
>
> *"Since his father left, I have tried to instill boundaries in Jake's life, but he is a strong-willed child. I think I get more peace by just leaving him alone at times."*
>
> *"He needs a man in his life to be sure."*

The scolding and spanking that Jake received had little effect on changing his attitude. When the adults left the room, everything went back to business as usual. Jake had no respect for authority, especially anyone who tried to claim the role of his father. Joe, however, was convinced that Jake was just a young recruit to be broken. The war games Jake played in his basement were nothing compared to those he would wage with Joe. Jake's bedroom became a safe haven, as well as a strategic planning location. If Jake interpreted love as any form of punishment, then he felt loved from Joe almost daily. How sad, if that is the only form of love Jake knew from anyone in authority in his life. Yet, it is comforting to know that Joan and Bob demonstrated love, however foreign, to Jake.

For several months, Joe would make regular visits. Each time Jake would be sent to his room. Mom did not desire to hear or witness the waging battle between them. Jake knew this only too well and bribed his mother for snacks, games, and other items, which further decreased the size of his bedroom. He developed the skill of manipulation and used it well. I can visualize a conversation with his mom going something like this:

> *"Joe is coming over tonight, Jake. Please try to be nice to him."*
>
> *"But mama, Joe was here last night and the night before."*

"I like him and he makes momma feel good."
"You work all day and don't spend any time with me."
"That's not true, Jake. Didn't I take you to the toy store on Saturday?"
"Yeah, and you complained about everything I touched there."
"Mom's just lonely."
"I'm here mom. Maybe we could play some games together."
"What games do you have in mind?"
"Chutes and Ladders would be good." (Jake knew that his choice would take a while. He played it once with her and she took the time to help him understand the rules)
"How about a game of hide-and-seek?"
"I'm six years old now. I am not a kid anymore."
"I keep forgetting that. Can't you just be a good boy and play in your room tonight, Jake?"
"I could play a long time if I had new joy sticks for my Atari game."
"If I bought you that, would you play in your room?"

Jake paused for a moment and then responded with an enthusiastic "sure."

"Okay Jake. I will have Joe pick it up on his way over."
"Have him pick up a can of popcorn as well. You know, the one with the cheese and other flavors."
"We have plenty of snacks here."
"You want me to play by myself all night?"
"Okay, okay I will see what I can do."

Jake knew every button to press. It was more than a game with him. It defined who he was, and who he would become. Joe was a big man. His military training and authoritative style became a formidable foe. Somehow, Jake relished the task of taking Joe on one-on-one. This also played a huge role in Jake's development. It was like David against Goliath, and the young boy would come out on top.

Joe tied the knot with Jake's mom before Jake turned seven. It seemed rather sudden, but Joe had received orders to relocate to Pearl Harbor in Hawaii. The concept of taking on a new father figure in his life may have sent sharp pains up Jake's spine. The idea of moving out of that apartment to Hawaii was a huge counterweight. Jake may have envisioned a new wonderland to explore, a chance to meet new friends, or playing in the sand on a warm beach. He may have wondered what it would be like to live where a cold day meant temperatures in the fifties, unlike the heavy snowfalls of the Northeast. Perhaps, his thoughts were on the new war games that he could play with his new father.

The ceremony was private. Before Jake knew it, he was packing for a trip across the ocean. Mom had kept everything from him until the last minute for fear of Jake's reaction. Joe took advantage of the army's generosity, and his new family began a new beginning in a land filled with volcanic sediment. How fitting that sounds as I look back on it now. Jake's life was full of chaos and an eruption could come at any time without warning.

Leaving that apartment was a sad event as well. Jimmy and his parents offered a true safe haven. The boys would have their share of misdemeanors, but still felt loved and accepted. Jake enjoyed tossing a ball with Bob as well, when he came home from work. Joan, Bob and Jimmy spent time together sharing with Jake about the move. They agreed to stay in touch and, if they could afford it someday, they would travel to the islands to visit. The two years in the apartment held some fond memories for Jake. Yet, when I counseled Jake about those times, he was quick to recall the incident with the painted stairs. Of all the positive moments that might have been mentioned, the multi-colored stairs held the top spot in his memory.

I can only wonder what takes place inside a boy's head, when one negative one overshadows a hundred good events. That was the case for Jake many years later. Hawaii has always been considered a paradise by mainlanders, but that would not be true for Jake. Leaving Jimmy and his family was not easy. The role models Bob and Joan demonstrated, as parents, were lost, except for an occasional postcard or letter. The painted steps were beautiful to Jake at the time he completed the task, much like the fliers of the Hawaiian Islands. But, beauty is a relative thing. The stairway offered a different impression to Jake's mom. Hawaii would also lose its splendor.

Still, Jake once again had a family, which included a father in his life. Joe was good to Jake's mom, and Jake at least acknowledged that. His mother often showed genuine joy in Joe's presence, and also enjoyed not having to work as a waitress any more. Joe's income may not have been great, but the benefits of military life seemed to compensate. The base offered very reasonable pricing in the Commissary along with free medical and dental plans. Hawaii was considered a tourist area with higher costs for basic essentials, but the army base easily compensated.

So off they went. The trip was a long one, yet everyone was filled with excitement. For Jake, it was his first time on an airplane. He sat by the window and enjoyed the view. First, they landed in Los Angeles, California, where they changed planes. This time it was a double-decker 747 with five additional seats in the middle. The cabin area was much larger than the apartment they were leaving, at least to Jake. Jake wrote a letter about the flight as best a seven-year-old could <u>muster and mailed</u> it to Jimmy after they reached the islands.

> *"Mama, have you ever seen water that blue?"*
> *"No Jake. It sure is beautiful."*
> *"I see some islands, mom. Look! Over there."*
> *"Sure looks small from up here, doesn't it Jake?"*
> *"Looks more like rocks."*
> *"As we get closer, they become pretty big rocks, Jake. That's where we are going to live for a while."*

Jake paused and thought about his new home. All that he could see for hours on the flight was blue water. His new home would be isolated from the mainland. He could not jump on his two-wheeler and pedal over to Jimmy's house. Yet, there was something about the islands that pleased him. Perhaps, it was the warm sunshine or the new things to discover.

The plane touched down, lightly jerking Jake backwards in his seat. *"We're here, Jake,"* mom exclaimed. Jake peered out the window and saw other planes parked in the distance. As the jet taxied into position, he observed workers wearing multi-colored clothing with dark tanned skin. Soon the passengers were let off the plane and greeted by women wearing grass skirts, handing out necklaces made of flowers. Jake shrugged away when a lei was about to be placed around his neck.

> *"Boys don't wear flow'rs, mama"*
> *Be nice, Jake. These people just want to be friendly."*

"How 'bout some shells instead," Jake snickered. Then he allowed one of the natives to place a string of flowers on his neck.

"Aloha," the lady added.

"A low who?" Jake replied. *"It appears as though they talk funny too."*

"We will have a lot of new things to learn while we are here, Jake."

With that, everyone proceeded to locate their luggage.

HAOLE

Tourists to the islands are welcomed by warm greetings, friendly smiles, and courteous treatment. Coming there to live was quite different, however. Jake began to attend school and found it difficult to make friends. Perhaps, the fire in his belly from losing a father still lingered and was negatively sensed by the other children. The Hawaiian slang term for a Caucasian person is Haole, pronounced "hool ee." Jake would hear this term along with various adjectives to enhance the meaning. The lush paradise was also filled with a dark side and Jake would be drawn inside.

Jake's new home was inside an extinct volcano. He had never seen anything like it before. His curiosity ignited his quest for new excitement. Playing war games in a volcano was much more invigorating than the small basement of his previous home. Of course, it would be far better to play with new friends, which Jake would find difficult to make as an outsider. Native Hawaiians did not look very favorably on Haoles trying to integrate into their culture. Jake would find this fact out soon enough.

> *"Hey Haolee,"* one native boy yelled out.
> *"You talkin' to me,"* Jake replied.
> *"Yeah, I'm talkin' to you, you stupid Haole."*
> *"Who you calling stupid, you yeller brillo pad?"* Jake said this because the boy's hair was dark and curly, along with his dark complexion.

Conversations like this earmarked Jake's two-year stay on the islands. Needless to say, he would have his share of bloody noses, cuts, black eyes, and scrapes. Each time he would come home, Joe would read the riot act to Jake.

> *"Who did you tick off today, Jake?"* Joe had a way of placing the blame on Jake for all confrontations.
> *"I just thought my nose needed ta match my other features,"* Jake answered with a touch of disrespect.
> *"If you think you need cosmetic changes, I would be more than happy to help you myself, you need to try and get along with the people here, Jake."*
> *"What for. They hate us hoolees. I don't have their yeller skin or briller pad hair. Maybe if they keep hitting me at the beaches, I will begin to look like them,"* Jake cynically responded.

Conversations like this were so common that Joe just turned away. There was no sense in continuing in the discussion any further. The relationship between Joe and Jake would not get any better during that time on the island. Jake came and went as he pleased while Joe was working. Fighting with the locals was a daily event, but something inside of Jake actually enjoyed the skirmishes. He may take on some cuts and bruises, but one good strike against the enemy brought such a rush. He began to get a new sense of power from the adrenalin rush. Fear became his strength. The bigger they were, the more euphoric the experience, even to a six year old child.

After a month on the islands, Jake received a letter from the mainland. His mother called to him outside the back door, when it arrived.

> *"Jake, you have mail."* *"Who's it from?"*
> *"Jimmy, Jimmy Randolph."*
> *"Jimmy? How'd he know where I live?"*
> *"I have been staying in touch with the family since we got here. Remember, we also sent the letter that you wrote on the plane?"*
> *"Oh yeah."*
> *"This letter seems to be written in Jimmy's handwriting."*

He ran to the house to get the letter. It was the first time anyone had written to him personally. He stared for several seconds at the envelope before opening it. During that time, mom grinned. She sensed the impact that it had on her son. Someone cared enough to send a personal greeting, and both mom and son were caught in a moment of euphoria. He carefully began to break the seal on the envelope, unlike tearing into a Christmas present. Mom, whose eyes reddened by a stream of tears, also noted his methodical actions.

Jake removed the letter and unfolded it with a similar manner. The words were rather largely printed in pencil. The letter read:

> Hi Jake.
> I hope U are having fun in Ha-
> waii.
> I miss U.
> U are my best frend.
> Luv
> Jimmy

The letter was short, but not to Jake who understood far more than the words that were written. He enjoyed the entire Randolph family, but leaving Jimmy was especially difficult. He was reminded that he had at least one friend, even if he was thousands of miles away. The letter was a treasure that touched the heart of a young boy. Jake wanted to let his best friend know and wrote these words on a small sheet of paper:

> Jimmy
> Its hot here and I miss U.
> Luv
> Jake
> *"Please send this to Jimmy, momma."*

It was a tender moment in her heart. The first weeks in Hawaii were filled with more unrest and dissension, but the letter provided a glimmer of hope. Jake's mom wrote a long response to the Randolph's and included Jake's letter. The expressions of a six-year-old had a profound impact.

The islands became a place for continuous learning. The people there talk funny, dress different, act strange, and have a different attitude towards those, who take up residence and try to change it. Jake stood out like a watermelon in a pumpkin patch by his mannerisms. Finding a friend like Jimmy seemed impossible. The lush foliage and warm climate offered little to help Jake shake his feelings of loneliness. He would often retreat to his bedroom and reread the short letter from his friend on the mainland. Somehow, it gave Jake a sense of peace, if only for a moment.

He was not about to anguish over things out of his control. The times that he would retreat to his room diminished as each new day passed. Facing the wrath of unfriendly natives became a challenge. The islands had a wealth of uncharted areas to discover. He was not about to let anyone stop him from seeking the treasures that lurked. Slowly, the natives began to accept him. They would dish out their barrage of insults, but Jake fired back with some retorts of his own. The exchange became his welcoming.

Jake's unwillingness to not back down from a confrontation won him some respect from the natives. His temper and quick mouth would still promote fights, but a few young boys began to enjoy hanging out with him. Each day to them was a new experience, as they wondered what trouble lay around the bend. Though they were under the age of ten, they had the bully mentality and Jake became their ringleader. The small gang of juveniles would purposefully run down the beaches, kicking up the dark colored lava sand on sunbathers, hoping to cause a reaction. It was as if the war games inside the volcano were being played with vacationers. The gang especially enjoyed stirring up trouble with visitors, almost as if Jake was now a native. The islands of paradise had a few troublemakers and Jake was lured to them like a magnet.

Paradise had taken on a new meaning for Jake. The beauty of the waterfalls and lush foliage may have been memorable for other visitors, but not for him. The painted steps of his last apartment had dimmed his sensitivity to the vibrant colors on the hillsides. The dark walls inside the extinct volcano offered far more excitement. He saw far more beauty with each new scar on his body.

On several occasions, Jake and his friends would take on the huge waves of the surf. Initially, he would just watch as surfers attempted to navigate the waves upright on their boards. When the crashing wave overtook a rider, Jake's heart pounded with excitement. He was far more interested in watching those who would resurface after the wave passed. When arms would rise with a sign of victory after being crushed, Jake seemed to raise his arm as well. He would have many opportunities to experience the thrill for himself, as his surfing technique left much to be desired. He would paddle out against the surf with the hopes of tackling the highest wave. Surviving was his goal and Jake was fearless in each attempt. On those occasions when he actually stayed on the board, I think he must have felt less fulfilled.

The homes inside the volcano were built like steps going up the rough terrain. The front door opened up at ground level, while the back of the house was often fifteen to twenty feet suspended over the lava rock below. This lower area became Jake's battlefield and getaway area. Kali, enjoyed playing with Jake in the back yard.

> *"What'ya got there Jake?"*
> *"One of my dad's lighters"*
> *"Let's make a fire."*
> *"Go find a lot of dried leaves, Kali. This is a perfect spot and no one will see us."*

Jake may have been told not to play with dad's lighters. Somehow he knew that starting a fire went against the family rules, or he would not have been so concerned about having anyone see them. The two boys scurried to find various kindling. The idea of watching a fire in that otherwise dark slope seemed like a great idea. He began to light a small pile of dried leaves. Before long, the pile grew larger with twigs and branches added. The fire began to grow out of control.

> *"Aiā!"* (Hawaiian for surprise when something goes wrong)

The fire was raging out of control and Kali freaked out.

> *"We can put it out, Kali."*
> *"Ahahana!"* (Hawaiian for, "You're going to get it.") *"I'm outta here."*

An eight-year-old boy is not blessed with great wisdom. At least that was the case for Jake. All he could think to do was to start stomping on the fire in an effort to put it out. With each plunge, the sparks flew in all directions. He may have given the appearance of playing hopscotch, as he jumped towards each new sighting of fire. Eventually, the fire was put out. The charred remains left obvious indications that a fire had been there. Jake would later recall this incident with alarming clarity. It was the first time that he had felt the rush of being bad and how to deal with real trouble, REAL trouble. The feeling would stay with him throughout his life.

As his parole officer, I understand how the islands may have affected his thoughts and actions. As a young boy, he lacked discipline and boundaries. The sudden exit of his father from his life was a blow to be sure. I wonder how anyone can truly understand the concepts of love, affection, and the joy they bring, when deprived of these emotions at such a young age. Hawaii may have been paradise for his mom, but Jake found a darker side there.

On the islands Jake was introduced to the concept of fear in a big way. Initially, fear was a useful developmental tool in his life. Yet, somehow, it became a welcomed friend. The rush he felt, whenever he was in the midst of danger, began to drive him into seeking trouble, rather than avoiding it. There was something about the thrill of danger, which drew him into more and more trouble. If fear was a drug, then Jake was hooked. Many parents use the concept of fear to teach their children to avoid touching a hot stove or accepting a ride from a stranger. To Jake, getting burned or abused was a necessary byproduct.

Neighborhood bullies might use their size to solicit the turn tail and run response, but not with Jake. Sometimes, he would stand and take his beating. At other times, the bullies met their match and became the ones who left. Jake may have felt some strength in numbers hanging with friends, but he developed the self-awareness, that he could handle himself alone against odds that appeared formidable. Whether or not he would get a beating was not on his mind. He would get in his licks and would not be intimidated by anyone. Hawaii was a training ground to be sure.

During my sessions with Jake as his parole officer, I would ask him about his tour in Hawaii. He answered:

"That was where I learned that I could take care of myself."

As I look back on his life, I see that the islands isolated him from the world in a way. He was a bit like Robinson Crusoe on a strange place, except he could communicate, at least to a degree. Nevertheless, I could not help but wonder why his journey took him there.

BACK TO THE MAINLAND

Joe's tour of duty in Hawaii came to an end and he was transferred back to an army base in Norfolk, Virginia. The name-calling and other forms of dissension had stopped. Now He would have to uproot and establish new friends. The lessons he learned on the islands would now influence him on the mainland, starting with the school system there. Norfolk in the eighties had two predominantly separate groups, namely "Blacks" and "Whites." These groups took on a defensive posture for their own turf, and Jake quickly realized that he needed to become connected with others to survive being "jumped." Respect was something to be earned all over again.

Home for Jake was now a third floor apartment with a view of a manufacturing plant, along with its pungent odor. Keeping the windows closed to avoid the smell also meant enduring the high summer heat, as the air conditioning unit had not worked for some time. That area of town was along a river and would be considered a slum zone by today's standards. Army pay was a limiting factor in finding suitable housing, and this rundown section of the city was now home. It was a far cry from the Hawaiian paradise to be sure.

School was a bus ride away. Segregation had found its way into the Virginia school system and Jake was now in the minority. He stood out like salt in a room full of pepper shakers. The new turf was established, and he would be thrust into survival mode. The daily beating attempts became commonplace until Aaron came along. Aaron was a scrappy white boy with some sort of inner suicidal desire. Jake was about to be beaten to a pulp by a gang of black boys twice his size, when Aaron jumped in between them and Jake.

"You boys want a piece of me, too?"
"This ain't your concern, white trash."
"I'm making it my concern, you over grown ape."

As one boy started towards Aaron, with a desire to make him eat his words, the others pulled him back. *"He ain't worth the effort. Let him have his new white trash friend."*

"This was not your fight. Why did you help me?"
"The odds did not look good in your favor, don't you think?"
"So two against six is more even?" Jake said with a snicker.
"Must be. They left didn't they?"
"Yeah!"

Jake appeared puzzled by the experience. Why did they leave? Aaron did not appear to have special martial arts skills, and his size was far less intimidating. The gang could have pulverized both of them. Nevertheless, Jake made a friend that day, a blood friend.

"What's your name?"
"My friends call me Aaron. What's yours?"
"I was born as Jonathan, but everyone calls me Jake."
"Jake it is then. Are you new here? I haven't seen you around."
"We were transferred here last month. The army relocated us from Hawaii."
"Hawaii. Wow! That must have been a big disappointment for you, Jake."
"I had some issues there, but it was okay. I guess we have a different native population here, huh?"
"Depends on what side of town you live. This is black turf."
"So why are you livin' here?"
"Mom can't afford anything better, since dad passed."
"What happened to your father, Aaron?"
"Mom says he got sick working at the factory, but I think he was murdered. I was only four. I barely remember him. That was six years ago."
"Murdered? Why would you think that?"
"Turf wars go on in factories too, Jake. I have learned to take a stand, despite the circumstances."

"Like you did for me?"
"I guess you could say that. It sure looked like you needed some help."
"I could have handled one or two, but six was a bit much. Anyway, thanks."

Jake couldn't help but see some of the similarities between Aaron and himself. Jake's father left when he was about the same age, though he did not die. Although his mother remarried, there were several years where Jake had to live in meager conditions. He had to fend for himself in Hawaii as a haole, like Aaron in the black section of town here. The thoughts would stay with him for some time, but not as long as the impression Aaron made on him. Jumping in to help a total stranger took guts. Aaron seemed to have that inner fortitude that would raise him above any situation. Jake was determined to find that for himself.

The days and weeks went by, and he made it a point to make contact with Aaron every day. They developed a strong bond between them. Aaron would introduce other white boys in the area. Home for Jake was with his new friends. They were his first associated gang. They called themselves the "River Rats." Fighting became a way of life. Rarely, would anyone fight battles alone. Jake was no longer a loner. Now he was part of a gang. He found new strength fighting in numbers. He would not back down from any altercation involving "Rats."

The River Rats had a mischievous side as well. When they were not busy tending to the battle scars, they would plan various petty crimes to do. The dark side had taken on a new form for Jake. Though the oldest gang member was barely thirteen, stealing a car for a joy ride was pretty common. They would start looking for vehicles with the keys still in the ignition, especially convertibles. Often people would carelessly run into the corner store for cigarettes and leave their cars idling. The scene was too hard to pass up. On several occasions, they would return the car before the owner ever came out of the store. The thrill of getting away with the act was like an endorphin rush.

Jake vividly remembered one time, when a lady came out to get into her car after buying a few items in the corner store. Her previously clean car was suddenly caked with mud. The gang had taken it for a spin through the muddy open field areas near the river. The tires spun out numerous times, causing mud to splatter everywhere. The light-colored vehicle was nearly unrecognizable. The look of disgust on the woman's face was a source of exhilaration for each gang member's. Although she looked around to see if an officer was in the area, she finally just got into her car and drove away. All anyone in the group needed to say was "mud" or "the look" and members of the gang would break out in uncontrollable laughter. The thought would instill new ideas on how to repeat similar events.

Joy rides later became burglaries as tape players hit the black market for petty cash. Money was the root of all evil for those who did not have it. Cigarettes, drugs, alcohol, and other illegal commodities could be bought on the street as long as you had the cash. Street dealers rarely checked IDs. Money talked. Whenever the River Rats wanted money, they would turn to breaking and entering houses. Often, they would find alcohol or drug items as well. They were a rag-tag band of bad kids, but they had each other. They were now the family that Jake had lacked, especially after his dad left. "I got you're back" was their blood oath. Jake would not back down from a confrontation or ever leave a brother in harms way. Joe may have learned this concept from his military training, but Jake found new strength in loyalty to his friends. In many ways, he came out of each skirmish with a sense of invincibility. Battle scars only seemed to enhance his feelings. His fearlessness was well received by the River Rats. Somehow, this band of juveniles became the family he never had, and he loved them.

He knew that it was wrong to steal. Yet, the rush that he felt while doing the act had become addictive. If the gang decided to go through with it, he was not going to let them down. Was it the thought that he had gotten away with something that he knew was wrong, that excited him? He was barely ten years old and this was now the life he knew. Petty crime, fighting, and disobedience were Jake's trademarks. He was definitely not a momma's boy.

On one occasion, he was staying at his friend David's house. Their mom's were out, so the two boys decided to build a bomb together. They had created rockets together using match heads inside small pepper cans in the past, but this time they went a bit further. Lighter fluid became the new ingredient along with a pen. They gutted the pen and filled it with the fluid. The pen was lit and thrown out the back door towards the yard. They anticipated some form of sonic boom, but no explosion took place. Instead, the dead grass caught fire. It quickly spread into the large courtyard nearby, with several houses in the area.

The fire behind his home in Hawaii instantly came to Jake's mind. He knew that jumping on it to put it out would be fruitless, so he ran to get the garden hose coiled by the house. The water was turned on and the pressure came full blast. By the time the fire was out, firemen arrived. The water had drenched the home's new carpet, along with muddy debris. The firemen approached the soot-covered boys with eyes that seemed to pierce beyond their appearance.

> *"How'd the fire start boys?"*
> *"I don't know. Do you know Dave?" "No, I don't know, Jake."*
> *"We saw it burning and quickly ran to get the hose to put it out,"* the two said almost in unison.

The firemen did not buy it for an instant and the two boys were escorted by the military police (MPs) to the police station. Once again, Jake felt the rush of being caught in an unlawful act. Joe had to come down to the station and pick Jake up, which brought heavy flack from Joe's superiors. It was one thing for Jake to get caught and quite another for his stepfather to get the blunt of the retribution. Needless to say, Jake would not escape due punishment later. This was the first of many run-ins with the law, which Jake would experience.

As Jake's parole officer years later, he would always bring up the euphoric high that he felt concerning the fires in Hawaii and Virginia. It was like a rush of adrenalin to a runner, which produced that sudden burst of energy to complete the race. He not only enjoyed the feeling, but he sought it. Playing stickball in the empty lot may have been fun for other boys, but not Jake. Somehow, the thrill of facing danger took on new heights of satisfaction. He found something that pulled him from the despair of losing a father. He didn't need anyone else to spur his confidence, just a moment of exhilaration from knowing he had met danger head on and came through more alive than ever. Jake knew right from wrong. Yet, each time he crossed the line, something clicked inside him. It was a feeling that Jake yearned. I could read it in his face whenever we discussed such matters.

He was not enamored with traditional family values and love. When his father left, mom had to find work to pay the bills. The weight of financial responsibility fell heavy on his mother, and he felt her worry and concern when she came home. Joe's presence later became a welcomed relief. He may have felt more like a liability than a son. The years that passed did little to instill love and affection from his parents. Joe was a typical toe-the-line army man. The need for conversation usually came in the form of discipline. Jake learned the art of manipulation. It became another form of facing a challenge and coming out on top. Joe may have thought he was in control, but it was Jake who held the reins.

Joe was also considering retirement from the military. He had twenty years of service and the idea of finding a place to set up permanent roots was appealing. Florida was a haven for lower income people like him, and quickly became the dream location. The weather in Hawaii was much preferred over all of the other places Joe had served. Florida seemed similar. The idea offered other positive opportunities as the racial wars in Virginia had taken a toll on the quality of education for Jake. Surely, the Sunshine State would offer a better venue.

The first five years of a boy's life often set the stage for scenes played out later. Jake could not remember much, but his father's sudden exit from his life was one area that jumped out when you ask him about those years. The nurturing of a father is especially important during elementary school. The art of throwing a baseball in the yard or going fishing at the local pond could have instilled those interests for years to come. Male bonding is important. The only form of that for Jake came through those he met at school or in the neighborhood, as his new father did not fare well in bridging the emotional or physical gap in Jake.

His mother may have tried to take on both the role of a mom and a father, but with little success. The things Jake could manipulate from both his mom and Joe was the only form of love he knew. A young child learns more about how to win than developing good character traits, which could benefit him or her later when faced with tough choices. Friends had a much higher influence on Jake when it comes to his value system. The years spent in Virginia proved to be a training ground for loyalty, respect, and manhood. These years did little to develop character traits of compassion, empathy, or forgiveness. He learned to depend on himself, if he was to survive.

Spiritual things were virtually non-existent. Any idea that God had a special plan for Jake, or that He loved him more than anyone else possibly could, was beyond comprehension. The hand that he was dealt was what it was and nothing more. He would just have to make the best of it. If anyone had his back, it was his friends. He would never let them down.

The black versus white mentality permeated most of Virginia and the country for that matter. The concept of protecting your turf in Virginia seemed to come from the black community with its weatherworn buildings, rusted basketball hoops without netting, and run down looking vehicles. Flower gardens, fancy homes, and swimming pools were most likely on the white side of the tracks. Due to a military salary, Jake experienced what it was like to live in a predominantly black community. He may not have understood much about the preconceived affluence on the other side, but he learned something about protecting what you do have.

Then there was also that dream, which would change the circumstances. Although he was still a child, he saw crime as a means to an end. Stealing from the rich sounded as normal as apple pie. Enjoying a joy ride, or other events attributed to a wealthy society, could easily be justified. For Jake, it was not a black versus white battle. Rather, it was more of a rich against poor quest. He was easily influenced by any conversation with his friends that involved living like those on the other side of the street. To escape from the life they were dealt, even for a short time, was a welcomed relief. Money was a means to buy drugs or alcohol. The River Rats became a closely-knit band of brothers.

THE BROTHER

Jake developed a special bond with Aaron who was the seventh child of aging parents. He was about ten when they met and a few months older than Jake. His mom was in her late forties when he was born and his dad died when he was four. He had pretty much the same freedoms as Jake when it came to getting away from home. Jake could count on him to meet him at the river anytime of day or night, without a lot of notice. Often Aaron would come to Jake's house to eat with his family, play games, and any other activities that were planned. Aaron was like family.

During one of those family gathering times, Aaron was sitting across from Jake having hotdogs and beans. Jake took a bite of his food and momentarily looked up towards Aaron. In that instant a missile hit him square in his left eye. Aaron used a fork to catapult a piece of hotdog in Jake's direction. It happened to be a direct hit. "You Dawg," Jake cried out. When he saw that the object that struck his eye was a hotdog, he started laughing. Aaron could not help from laughing as well. From that point on Aaron had the name, "Dawg." It was like a humorous reminder of the incident. Jake's mother and stepfather were ready to scold Aaron for his foolishness, but the two boys were laughing so hard, that they held their peace.

One day, Jake went out to meet his friend at the river, but Dawg did not show. He waited for almost an hour before deciding to trek on over to Dawg's house. There were many cars in the driveway and on the street, indicating that something had happened. Jake spotted his friend and called out to him.

"Hey Dawg. What's goin on?"

"They took mom to the hospital. I think she had a heart attack."
"Is anyone from your family here?"
"No. My older sister was here, but she went in the ambulance."
"So who are all these people?"
"Friends, neighbors, and relatives."
"Your family has a lot of friends. If this happened to my family,
I think I could count on one hand the number of people who
would stop by."
"Yeah! We always had people around. I guess seven kids will do
that to a family."
"I guess you're right. I wouldn't know."

Jake stayed with his friend for most of the night; long after the other guests had left. The two were hoping for some good news. For that moment in time, they were caught up in the reality of life. They did not think about going out to cause some mischievous act. Dawg was hurting and Jake wanted to be there for him. It was an emotional experience for Jake, which he had not felt before. It was a brief defining moment in his life.

The only experience that came close involved his grandfather (mother's father), whom he affectionately referred to as "Papa." Jake was about three when his pet guinea pig, named Furball, was found motionless in its cage. He was heartbroken. Furball was a gift on his third birthday. The two had a great relationship. He would take him out of his cage regularly for feeding. Furball gently ate cabbage from his hand and was especially fond of carrots. Jake's room was often a get away place and Furball was a welcomed friend. Papa stopped by on the day Furball died and spent most of the day listening to Jake's broken heart. Now Jake was doing that for his friend Dawg.

Aaron was like an only child at that point in his life, as his six siblings were no longer staying at home. When the ambulance was called, he was en route to meet up with Jake at the river. Aaron's sister asked a neighbor to go down to the river and let her brother know that they were leaving for the hospital. The neighbor caught up to Aaron, before he met up with Jake, to give him the news, and the two of them made a u-turn back to the house. By the time Aaron got there, the ambulance had left. The neighbors did their best to comfort him, but they knew the attack was far more serious.

The two boys sat and talked on the front steps of Dawg's home for hours. The discussion centered on feelings and thoughts that were foremost on Aaron's mind. Jake offered little thoughts or feelings of his own. Usually, he took control of a conversation, as he would do with his parents, but not this time. He became a listener. It was a new experience for him.

> *"What am I going to do if mom dies, Jake?"*
> *"You'll get by, Dawg."*
> *"My brothers and sisters have homes of their own and I don't want to be a burden on them."*
> *"Do you have an aunt or uncle to live with?"*
> *"Most of them live outside the state. I know this area is not the best, but I like it here."*
> *"You could always live with me, Dawg."*

Aaron appeared to stop communicating. Could he leave his family and live with Jake? Was that even a possibility The emotions felt that night were strong and powerful. It was as if Jake was his new little brother. A sense of hope came over Aaron. His sister did not come home that night. She tried to call the house, but in the commotion the phone had been left off the hook. Cell phones were not invented yet, and the boys did not go inside the house all night. Somehow, neither Jake nor Dawg wanted to face anything inside. About two in the morning the two boys decided to leave and go to Jake's house. His parents were in bed, so they quietly went to Jake's room and fell asleep.

The next morning Jake came downstairs. It was summertime and school was out. Sleeping late was part of the normal daily event. Jake's mom was busy preparing a large pot of stew for the evening meal. His stepfather was having coffee on the front porch, so Jake felt the urge to approach his mother with the news about his friend.

> *"Mom. Did you know I came home late last night?"*
> *"We went to bed about midnight and I knew you were not home before that. I heard something about three or so. Was that you?"*
> *"Yes. But I was not alone. Dawg came home with me."*
> *"Is he here now?"*

"Yes. His mom was taken to the hospital last night around seven. Neighbors said it was a heart attack."
"That's terrible. Is she all right?"
"We waited until about two this morning and did not hear anything, so we came here."
"I will call there to get an update."

Jake's mom dialed Aaron's number. Yes, I said, "dialed" as the modern pushbutton telephone had not yet reached their household. The line had a busy signal. Aaron's mom or sister did come home that night and the phone was still off the hook. Aaron came down the steps from Jake's room and Jake's mom ran to him.

"I am so sorry about your mom. I pray that she will be okay."
"Yeah! Fifty-five isn't that old, is it?"
"No, Jake. People live well into their eighties and nineties."
"Thanks for letting me stay with Jake last night. He is a great friend."
"I'm so proud of him for inviting you. You have been like family here."

Those words permeated Aaron's heart. Jake's mother did not know about the conversation the two boys had that evening. She knew that Aaron lost his father, as Jake shared that with her several weeks earlier. Jake also had a moment of sincere love from his mother. She was proud of him. Since his dad left, Jake might not have ever felt a sense of pride from his mother. His selfish antics to manipulate her were not intended to solicit a sense of pride. Yet, she was proud of her son for taking the action to invite a friend in need home with him. At that moment Jake felt much older than a twelve-year-old boy.

His mom went out and told her husband what had happened and the four of them decided to drive over to Aaron's house. When they arrived, no one was home. The hospital was just a mile away, so off they went. When they arrived, Aaron's sister was sobbing and clinging to her oldest daughter. The news of her mother's passing had just been given to the family. The timing could not have been worse for Aaron. It was bad enough to hear that he had just lost his mother, but to see his sister weeping so uncontrollably was more than he could bear. He ran out of the hospital ward. Jake ran after him, while his parents stayed to offer their support.

Jake caught up to his friend at the hospital entrance. He grabbed Dawg by the arm before he could leave.

> *"Wait, Dawg, wait."*
> *"What for? Mom is dead. My worst fears have been realized."*
> *"You still have me, Dawg."*
> *"What am I goin to do now?"*
> *"You can stay with us for now, Dawg"*
> *"I would love that, Jake. You are a good friend. First dad and now mom…"*
> *"You will be okay, Dawg. You will"*
> *"But I am twelve Jake. I'm almost a man."*
> *"You have a large family. I envy that."*
> *"I'm glad sis is here. I hate to see her leave."*
> *"Things will work out. You'll see."*
> *"I hope you are right, Jake."*

Jake remembered hearing those very words from Papa when Furball passed away. *"Everything will work out. You' ll see, Jake."* It was almost as if Papa was speaking to his friend at that moment. Papa was Jake's only child influence with strong Christian values. He always spoke out of love with such confidence. Jake thoroughly enjoyed Papa's visits, so much so that, he hated to see him leave. As his parole officer, I can remember many times when Jake said that he could never be the man his grandfather was. Yet, as I wait outside the courtroom, I can see a man across the atrium who has found the love and peace that his grandfather had.

The two of them proceeded to a cluster of chairs and couches in the hospital foyer. It was a time when they would draw even closer than they ever did before. The rest of the family spotted them as they were leaving the hospital. By this time, Aaron's sister had stopped her tears, but the evidence was still written on her face. She was deeply hurting. Aaron ran over to her and gave her an embrace that cried out, "I love you sis," though no words were spoken. His sister needed that.

The conversation about the future began to take place. Aaron was suddenly alone. There were no conversations about where he would go. His mother's heart attack came unannounced. Aaron wished that he had the time to share what he felt about his mom, while she was alive, but the moment was now gone forever. Aaron's sister was willing to take her brother back to Georgia, where she lived with her husband and two children, but there was too much to do there in Virginia. She could stay in the house for a while to get things in order, but... There were more "buts" than answers. Jake's mom told her that Aaron could stay with them. That brought some comfort to Aaron's sister as she truly dreaded the idea of spending even one night at her mother's home with all the memories there, at least not for a while. The plan was set in motion, and that night Aaron went to live with Jake.

Aaron's sister stayed in the area for several weeks to prepare the house for sale and pack up the artifacts. She would call every day to check on her brother and was always excited to hear how well he was doing. Aaron enjoyed talking to her as well. Slowly, the crackle in her voice turned to calmness. The grief she was bearing was still there, but her brother and others were bringing some comfort. Her biggest comfort, however, was the fact that Aaron was lovingly being cared for. She worried about that, but not any more. Now she had another brother named Jake.

After a few months had passed, the property was sold. Aaron's sister had been traveling between her home and her mother's home at least twice a month. Selling of the home was both sad and a relief. With each trip, she would visit Aaron and leave feeling good about the decision to leave him in the care of Jake's parents. The process of cleaning out the house solicited Aaron's help as well. Aaron was able to sort through some of the things in their home before everything was packed. He found a few artifacts that would remind him of his father, which he kept for himself.

One of them was a pocketknife with a curved four-inch blade. It would be a subject of conversation between him and Jake for a long time. He also found a World War II German luger and a few bullets. His dad had kept it as a souvenir from the war. He was drafted and served in the invasion at Normandy. Aaron did not let his sister know that he had taken the gun. His sister never knew about it anyway. The gun was hidden in a shoebox beneath a pile of other boxes, and Aaron was the first one sorting through that room. Once the war had ended, memories were buried as well by Aaron's father. The artifacts were only reminders of the utter travesty. The knife and luger would play a prominent role in Jake's life.

Jake and his parents talked about permanently adopting Aaron so that he could have the same privileges with school and other events. The legal implications were also examined and discussed with Aaron's sister. Just over a year after his mother passed, Aaron became Jake's adopted brother. Aaron's sister thought it would be best for her brother, as she had a full plate raising her own family. Besides, Aaron was in good hands. Jake's parents had proven that they genuinely cared for him, and his sister knew how much her brother cared about them.

The legal proceedings for adoption were completed almost as quickly as they began. In a few short months, Aaron became Jake's brother. When Aaron stepped in to help Jake from receiving a severe beating, he was a friend and blood brother. Now, Aaron was family. Life offers a lot of twists and turns, but nothing like the one that would happen as a result of this new union.

Life is much more than a series of aimless events. People live and die, but in between they seem to work their way through a maze. For some, the path takes them deeper into the unknown. Others find the path, which leads them out of the maze. Rarely, are any moves without purpose. We meet people along each direction. We hear words spoken or see events that have a profound impact on our lives. Jake's maze began when his father left. He traveled to Hawaii and now to Virginia. In each location he witnessed different forms of culture, made different friends, and had moments of extreme emotion. The journey continues, but now with a brother.

THE PRETEEN YEARS

The River Rats found a sense of family as they hung together. Aaron had developed his circle of friends and got involved with the "Rats" on rare occasions. The petty crimes were daily sources of adventure. Stealing was commonplace, but they were careful that no one got hurt, especially those in the homes they targeted. They carefully planned each event. A person was selected to watch the grounds, while two or three would break in. They would target well-to-do homes and justify their actions with words like, "They got insurance," or "They have so much that they won't miss a few items." Somehow, Jake believed each chant as if it was the truth.

By the time Jake turned twelve, he had a rap sheet of misdemeanors that would put an adult away for life. The court system was far more lenient to juveniles, however, and the customary slap on the hand became Jake's punishment. The measure of accountability was so light that for Jake crime did pay. It helped to have a military stepfather to keep the slap to a minimum. Their conversation after each trip to the police station went something like this:

> *"Jake, what did you do this time?"*
> *"We were playing ball near that house and Jose hit one through the window."* (He said that to justify why the window was broken.)
> *"What were you doing on that side of town anyway?"*
> *"Peter had a friend living near there, who invited us to play with him. We could always use more players."*
> *"You were caught coming out of the house with stolen property. Explain that to me."*

"Peter's friend said the stereo was his and the kid who lived there had borrowed it. Since we had to get inside to get the baseball anyway, Peter said we should get his equipment while there."
"Come on Jake. You believed him?"
"I didn't know what to believe. Peter said it was okay and he was my friend."
"Where do you come up with stories like this?"

Jake just shrugged his shoulders and did not respond.

"I think these boys are a bad influence on you, Jake. You need to stop hanging with them."
"But, Jose and Peter are my friends."
"Nevertheless, you are grounded for a week."

Conversations like this were ever so commonplace. Jake had mastered the art of ducking the issues and passing blame on someone else. The act of convincing Joe that he was a victim, brought a rush to Jake's inner being, a rush that made the crime worth it. Being caught red-handed and getting away with it brought back the same feelings as the fire in Hawaii and again in Virginia. It was his way of getting "high."

Joe never referred to Jake as "Son." And Jake did not call Joe, "Dad." Any expressions of love were only felt in the paddle each time Joe inflicted punishment. Jake did not express love in any form to Joe. He had not learned it from his father, or from his mother who felt betrayed after his father left. The concept of love was very foreign to him. The kinship of the River Rats was as close as it came. Any admonishment from Joe to stay clear of the River Rats was quickly ignored. After Joe left the house, everything was back to the way it was before.

By the time Jake was thirteen, he had tried various drugs, including marijuana. Older brothers of the members brought alcoholic beverages to the River Rat meeting places. Fake IDs were used by some of the older kids to make purchases with stolen monies. Jake would refer to those days as mischievous times. Break-ins were planned, but no weapons were used. No one inside was hurt. They were a bunch of misguided kids looking for something to do. Each time they would get away with a robbery, the next one came easier. Each time they were caught in the act, thoughts of larceny would be replaced with hanging out, drinking beer, and testing the drug scene. Perhaps, the alcohol and drugs numbed their senses enough, that planning a new crime became easier.

Jake remembers one skirmish, involving bloodshed. The River Rats were confronted by a group of black boys trying to expand their turf. They were considerably larger, but the River Rats screamed, "Bring it on." Fists began flying and the Rats were being overwhelmed. Jake remembers wrestling a baseball bat away from one of the gang members and wielded it toward an oppressor. The bat hit the boy across the right side of his head and blood gushed out. The scene was etched in his mind. A bloody nose was nothing, compared to the gusher coming from the boy's head. Jake thought he had killed the gang member. The fight came to a quick end as the other boys ran to their friend's aid.

A battle began to wage inside Jake's mind. The battle with the street gang would continue another day, but the idea that a boy may have been killed filled his conscious thoughts. It would have been one thing if the blow came from a fist, but a weapon was used. The thought of the bat striking the boy's head and the sudden rush of blood created a permanent and powerful image in his mind. It elevated the invincible feelings felt by the fires in Hawaii and Virginia. The bat was meant to put a hurt on the Rats, but in an instant became stained with the blood of the ones who brought it. One might think that might discourage bringing weaponry to a turf war, but Jake could not stop thinking about the power he felt in wielding it. He later learned that the boy had survived.

Shortly afterwards, Joe uprooted his family to Central Florida. A doublewide trailer awaited them. It was the first place they could actually call home. Joe relished the idea that he could retire in sunshine less than an hour from the beach, and have a place to actually own. The trailer was new and larger than any rental they had been in before. He had the freedom to work around the yard and the backyard shed became his palace. Everything had its place.

Joe also discussed the move with his wife as a way of getting Jake away from the turf wars of the north. Southern Florida was considered, but the beaches of Miami had become a haven for Cuban refugees, wild parties, and drugs. Living near Disney World sounded like the ideal place to bring family values to a thirteen year old. Everything looked great on the surface, but by then, all of Florida was a pipeline for drug traffic. Crime was much worse and misdemeanors may have been nothing compared with the common knives and gun crimes. The move may have appeared to be a positive one, but a darker side lurked.

Jake saw evidence of the life he would be a part of on his first day of school there. Although, knives and guns were banned from the school, there was little chance to prevent the items from surfacing. Several people offered drugs to Jake before anyone knew his name. Reading, writing, and arithmetic took second place to simply surviving each day at school. Surviving alone was nearly impossible, so he actively sought new friendships. The eighth grade seemed to be a testing ground for turning boys into young men. "I got your back," meant much more than it did in Virginia. Add to that the biological changes from puberty, and you have a brewing firestorm.

Selling pot in the eighth grade was rather routine. That age was a time of making friends and being part of a group. The hormones were raging and the search for identity became the primary focus. You either were a "goody-two-shoes" or you joined the respected "hip" group. Boys did not want to be viewed as wimps and tended to hang with the macho crowds. Life was nothing like Arthur Fonzerelli (The Fonz) and his soda shop friends from the TV show, "Happy Days" of the sixties, at least not in central Florida. Kids hung out in secret getaway places. Manhood was measured by how many beers you could get illegally. Respect was earned by the amount of contraband you could bring to the meetings.

Jake learned how to sell drugs to the weaker kids by disguising oregano as pot in small clear plastic bags. He knew that the kids could not do anything about being "ripped off." Jake was able to use the cash to buy real drugs, a cycle that would be repeated often. Money meant alcohol and drugs. Alcohol and drugs translated into power. Having dominion over ten to twelve year olds and the respect from peers was the only concept of love that he knew.

Patch sat next to Jake in his homeroom class. He had a birthmark on the side of his face that may have warranted the nickname. In any case, Jake would call him Patch with a measure of respect. The two would become good friends and hung together after school. Patch introduced Jake to other boys and before the first semester was over, they called themselves the "Orange Crush." Once again, Jake found himself in a gang.

He recalls one of the first crimes he committed with the Crush involving a burglary. The gang had cased a neighborhood with homes priced well above those owned by the average American. The gang watched both cars leave the home and determined that the time was right to break in and steal electronic gear, which held high value on the black market in Florida. Jake was one of the boys who entered the home, while others kept vigil outside. As the boys cased the house, they were unaware of a pet parrot caged in the living room. As they entered the room, they heard the rustling of feathers coming from the cage.

> *"What was that, Jake?"*
> *"It's just a parrot. I see the VCR and other equipment over there."*

The conversation continued as the boys entered the room and began lifting the VCR and stereo equipment. Jake eyed a quality Betamax Camcorder and thought briefly about removing it as well. Little did Jake know that the parrot and the camcorder would be his undoing. The recorder was active and the exploit was captured on tape. Jake was identified along with confirmation from the bird, who was screeching:

> *"What was that, Jake." "What was that, Jake." "What was that, Jake."*

The words came out very recognizable, and the officer in charge of the investigation had little difficulty writing them down. Less than a week later the police showed up at Jake's school. To avoid a scene, the principle called Jake out of class to come to his office. He was caught red-handed. Denial was not an option. All Jake could think of is that he should have followed through on taking the camcorder. We should learn from our mistakes. In his case, he committed a crime and could only think of how he could have gotten away with it. The parrot's words would have had little clout without the taped evidence. "If only he had taken the camcorder," was all Jake could think about. Although the police tried to get the names of the others involved, Jake would not rat on them. He received three months of detention and two years of probation.

Suddenly, the move to Florida as an escape from trouble became a new source of it. The military commanders were no longer part of the equation. Joe and his wife would deal with the issues without the high visibility of the army. Joe may have convinced his wife that Florida would be a better environment for Jake than the black versus white scene in Virginia, but in his heart he knew that was not true. He may not have known how bad the drug abuse was, but he knew from his military training that the enemy would be there. Eventually, a stand needed to be made. Avoidance was temporary at best.

School security was pretty much of a joke in the mid-eighties. Weapons, drugs, and other taboo items were as common inside the classrooms as the books they were studying.

"Look at this, Jake. I got it from my big brother"
"That's a great lookin' knife. Is it sharp?"
"You bet."
"How come you brought it in school?"
"Are you kidding? …for protection."
"From who?"
"You are new here, aren't you Jake?"
"Well, I…"
"People will try and give you drugs or get you to sell them. If you refuse, you are marked."
"Whataya mean marked?"
"Don't be naïve. This place is where you either fall into their trap or face the consequences."
"I'm not afraid. Let them try."
"That's the point, Jake. They will and you got to be ready for just about anything."
"That's why you brought the knife?"
"Yeah! Have you met Johnny yet?"
"Is he the scrawny kid that sits in the back of Miss Joan's class?"
"That's him. He refused to sell drugs and they cut him pretty bad. He missed almost a year of school."

"That explains the scars on his face and arms."
"It is also why he sits in the back of every class, and his mom picks him up every night from school."

Before the week was over, Jake began bringing a pocketknife to school. He found it in an old fishing tackle box that Joe had stored away. Joe had not done any fishing since he became Jake's stepfather. Perhaps, he fished with other soldiers before. Anyway, Jake knew that the knife would not be missed. It was pretty rusty and needed a lot of work, so he took on the task of restoration. The knife had a four-inch blade and a second one that was used for scaling fish. By the time he was finished with it, both blades sparkled better than new. The knife could open very quickly by a quick shake of the wrists, and you could shave with the main blade.

He had little trouble showing it off to his friends. The ease at which it could cut paper was impressive. Then the confrontation time happened, just as Jake was told it would. Upon leaving school one Friday afternoon, three older boys grabbed Jake and dragged him behind the school. They were considerably older and larger than Jake, with LSD as their commodity. Either Jake would become a client or a dealer. They didn't care which one he chose. The shorter and stocky one began to shove Jake to the ground, as if to generate fear and superiority, but Jake quickly jumped back up. He did not have his friends there to "watch his back," but he knew that he had to take a stand. A taller boy joined in with more shoving and, once again, Jake leaped back up. This time the pocketknife was opened in his right hand with the words, *" back off."*

One thing was certain, namely, they would not heed Jake's words.

"Whataya goin' to do with that pig stabber, boy?"
"Leave me alone or I will cut you."
"You got guts kid. We'll give you that, but who do you think you are dealin' with?"
"Sewer trash."

Jake was quick to spew words without fully understanding the consequences, and this was one of those times. By the time the dust cleared, Jake had a bloody nose, a cracked rib and multiple other bruises. Two of the boys bled from the cuts inflicted from the fishing knife, one of them seriously. The police had been called when a teacher heard the yelling. Jake was taken to the station and arraigned for knife possession on school property. His parents were brought in once again to sign the release forms. A night in the slammer may have been the better choice, but they were new residents and wanted a fresh start. This was not the kind they had in mind.

The fishing knife was confiscated by the police and no longer in Jake's possession. The knife was a symbol of power, especially when clenched firmly in his hand. It made him feel invincible. He faced unreasonable odds and came out victorious. It was as though the knife was the equalizer. Feelings like these became infectious and he would draw on them often. His mind began to focus on how to keep from being robbed again. Carrying a weapon for protection was the edge he needed, should someone try to overpower him.

Shortly after the weapon possession charge, Aaron approached him with a shoebox. Inside it were the knife and luger from his father.

> *"Hey Dawg! What's in the box?"*
> *"Take a look for yourself, Jake."*
> *"Wow! Cool stuff."*
> *"They belonged to my dad from the war."*
> *"Does the gun work?"*
> *"Yeah! It's a German luger. I cleaned it. You can shave with the knife as well."*
> *"Why are you showing these to me now, Dawg?"*
> *"I keep these hidden under some other boxes in my closet. I just thought you might like to see them. Sometimes I go out with one or both on me, especially when I know the place I am going to is unsafe. Mom is about to redo my room and I need a place to keep them so that she doesn't find them."*
> *"I will keep them in my closet, Dawg."*
> *"Thanks. I was hoping you would say that."*

The luger could not have come at a better time, as far as Jake was concerned. It provided the security he needed. Behind the closed door of his bedroom, he played war games. This time he had a real gun in his hands. He experimented with various storage techniques on his body. Carrying it with the cold steel barrel snug against the small of his back, gave him a sense of power. He spent many nights in his room fondling the gun and flipping the knife blade open. Although, the games played were make-believe, something inside him took on a more realistic sense.

Jake had a juvenile record starting around his thirteenth birthday. As his parole officer, I had regular weekly meetings and could see a young boy with a lot to overcome in his life. The loss of his father was, perhaps, the most devastating moment in his life. For the most part he was respectful to me during our meetings. "Yes sir," he would say routinely. His stepfather may have had an influence on that, but I always felt it was an honest attempt at being servant to authority. He was now turning fifteen. His body was developing muscle tone. He no longer had the boyish face and the scars from fighting were obvious reminders of where he had been. His two-year probation period was now over and I called Jake in to make it official. Although I could never prove he violated his parole time, I certainly suspected it. His life had too many obstacles and the friends he hung with were not schoolteachers.

The announcement of the end of probation triggered the need for a party. Jake and his friends gathered to celebrate. At three A.M. the illegally supplied cigarettes and alcohol ran out. Six of the boys decided to extend the party by robbing a local convenient store. The store was closed, but a well-placed brick against the front glass doors would solve that problem. Once inside, the gang began to load up with cigarettes, beer, and "slim jims." I suppose people do stupid things while under the influence of alcohol or drugs. Smashing the glass on the front of a store on a well lit street was not very smart as a passing patrol car spotted the broken glass and stopped. Out of the six boys, only one escaped and he was not Jake.

Less than twelve hours earlier, I had released him from his probation. Now he was starting a new series of sessions with me along with some detention time. The small jail cell for thirty days would be his new home. Mom and dad would not be able to help him this time. One can only imagine what went through his mind as he stared at the heavy steel bars around him. Society would hope that that time would be a wake-up call, but for those kids out there who receive love from each other and little from their families at home, life paints a different story. The bars may have felt more like protection against muggers, than punishment. The only things those boys missed were cigarettes, beer, and getting high.

I now had Jake for two more years. In many ways, I may have been more of a father to him than the one in his home. Our counseling sessions probed deep into Jake's head and heart. I wanted to help him in the worst way. The rewards of being a parole officer come when those under our supervision become servants in society. Crime had been Jake's way of life. The friends he had made came from similar broken homes. The concept of "Love" was not spent listening to books being read before bedtime. Discussions around the dinner table were more like yelling fests, and playing a game with mom and dad meant isolation in your room.

After release from jail, Jake was remanded to his room. Mom and dad could not enforce such an edict, and he reunited with his friends once again. The four walls of his room might have seemed like boundaries to his parents, but not to him. Windows were made to climb out. Once out, no boundaries could be seen. The jail cell had a different perspective. There were no escape routes. Once the doors closed, there was a sense of closure. The walls kept inside what was inside. The outside world did not exist to its prisoners, except in their minds. Jake's home was no jail cell. Perhaps, a touch of reality entered his life. At least he had time to reflect as the cell doors meant there was no quick exit like he e joyed at home.

THE TEENAGE YEARS

Florida was a major hub of drug trafficking, not limited to the ports. The inner cities in the state were now infested, especially the heavy tourist sites. What was once known as a family vacation Mecca has now become a breeding ground for drug lords and pimps. If you want to sell something, go where the money is. Jake was right in the middle of the most prolific drug trafficking in the state and, perhaps, the whole country. His eighth grade class taught far more about dealing drugs than reading, writing or arithmetic. A dime bag of weed would sell for ten dollars. He found out very quickly that you could invest thirty dollars for a quarter bag (about 7 grams) and turn it into seven dime bags netting a fast forty-dollar profit, as long as he didn't smoke it first. The money came much easier than breaking, entering, and stealing from the upscale neighborhoods. Once the habit started, grams became ounces and ounces turned to pounds. Selling drugs was a lucrative business. Before long, he was handling kilos of dope.

The business was not without setbacks as he was robbed at gunpoint numerous times. On one occasion, a man approached him with a shotgun hidden under his trench coat and demanded money. Jake had purchase four hundred dollars worth of pot from a dealer on credit. Normally, this would turn a quick profit and the debt would be repaid within twenty-four hours. Without product to sell, he needed to approach the dealer with the news that he had been robbed. Perhaps, he was hoping for some mercy, but that did not happen. The dealer pulled out a gun and demanded payment. You might be able to talk your way out of some things, but a double barrel shotgun does not have ears.

He ended up working off his debt doing roofing. Like many dealers, legitimate businesses are also fronts. The dealer's roofing business had been robbed at least twice. Police suspected the thieves were after far more than money, but found no evidence to substantiate their suspicions. Jake learned the roofing business, as it took all summer to repay the four hundred dollar debt. The experience may have been a good lesson in hard work and earning a living honestly for some people, but not for Jake. He knew that he could earn as much in a single night of drug running, than an entire summer of working.

Jake spelled probation, "PARTY." There was always a party somewhere. Hanging out with so-called friends was better than staying home and listening to his stepfather accusing him of being worthless. The movie, "Iron Eagle" with Lou Gossett momentarily inspired him to consider joining the military. He shared that ambition with his stepfather. The conversation went something like this:

> *"Did you see the movie, "Iron Eagle"?*
> *"Not yet. Maybe your mother and I can see it later this week."*
> *"You'll like it. A shot down pilot was captured and his son organized a group of teenagers to get him back."*
> *"Sounds more like science fiction to me."*
> *"Maybe so, but I liked it."*
> *"Doesn't sound like anything you could do with that rag-tag bunch of kids you hang with."*
> *"The movie might have been unrealistic, but I got caught up with the thrill."*
> *"So now you are a thrill seeker, huh?"*
> *"Maybe, but I think I should join the military after graduation."*
> *"First, you have to graduate, and that does not look too promising. Second, You're too stupid to pass the entrance test."*

Conversations of any kind with his stepfather were rare, but Jake recalled this one with great clarity. His stepfather had bailed him out more times than he could remember, so perhaps, the words fit. After all Jake did not seem to learn from his mistakes. Yet, the word, "stupid" stuck with Jake. It also placed another barrier between the father-son relationships. If Jake was too stupid to be in the military, then his stepfather was the smart man in that family, as the military accepted him. As his parole officer, I could only dream that he would enlist. Certainly, any armed services branch would make a huge difference in turning this boy around. He was on a path of self-destruction. The one hope for restoration was shot down with a single word, "stupid." That was one label that really haunted him, as he shared in many parole sessions.

Jake also enjoyed the movie, "Scarface," where Tony Montana was not considered to be very smart. But, he packed heat and used the power of positive thinking to elevate himself to respectability. It was a role that Jake began to model. The one moment of rational thinking, with respect to enlistment, was shot down and Tony Montana became his role model. A word of encouragement from his stepfather may have changed all that, but that did not happen. The adage, "Sticks and stones can break your bones, but names can never hurt you," was proven false that day. The name, "stupid" hurt deeply. His measure of intelligence would now be supported by the handgun pressed against his back. The conversation with his stepfather would also trigger additional thoughts about his future. Getting out from under the control of his stepfather was priority one.

The boys from his hood found strength hanging out together. It was their daily ritual. None of them held jobs. Working was for stiffs who were too stupid to find ways to support themselves and their habits any other way. One night, two of his "buddies" decided to rob a pizza shop. One of the boy's girl friends got scared and alerted the police. One boy waited outside, while the other ran in with his gun in hand. He saw the place swarming with cops and ran out the back door. The cops gave chase. The boy decided to turn around to see where the police were. The cops saw the gun in hand and opened fire. A twelve-gauge shotgun ended Jake's friend's life. The other boy was caught a block away. He was beaten so bad that he went to prison with two broken arms. Reality struck as Jake saw the consequences of a life of crime. It was the first time anyone in his gang was killed, and according to Jake, was not the last. The world of crime and drugs looked great for street kids, but death and prison was a grim reminder that the party can and will end someday.

Jake was almost seventeen when he met his first wife, Joy. The testosterone levels were high and girls offered a new source of thrills. Joy was married, but her husband was serving in the first Gulf War in Iraq. She had money and a car, which made Jake's life a whole lot easier. Jake never loved her and thought they would part company just before her husband came home. He was anxious to get away from his stepfather and moved in with Joy. He told his mother that he had gotten her pregnant and needed to take responsibility for his actions. The plan backfired. Shortly after he moved in, she did get pregnant. Suddenly, everything changed. When her husband found out, he divorced her quickly.

He was now a seventeen-year-old father. He did not have a clue about what a father should be. Nevertheless, he tried to clean up his act and go straight. Working for four dollars an hour in his words, "sucked." He knew he could make hundreds a day selling dope. By his son's first birthday, he was gone. His father left him and now he took the same course of action with his son. Fatherhood was taught to Jake in several ways. If you don't like the hand you are dealt, walk away. That was the message his father left him. His stepfather handed out every form of criticism without any encouraging words. His message was, *"You are a loser Jake. You will never account to anything."* Jake had mastered the art of living one day at a time. Tomorrow may never come, as he had seen firsthand with the deaths of hood members.

He had two motives for leaving his parents, namely, sex and separation from their authority. He did not see anything worthwhile from attending school. After all, he learned more there about drug handling or alcohol abuse, than any course of study. Thrill seeking came in either of those forms and also in the activities below the sheets. Sleeping with a married woman did not trigger a conscious response that it was wrong. Joy's sense of morality was also skewed. Her husband was thousands of miles away, so how would he know. Besides, the months of separation without an occasional thrill was a dismal thought. The two used each other to get what they wanted. If she had not gotten pregnant, one can only wonder what the outcome may have been like when her husband came home.

Nevertheless, Jake became caught up in a spiraling downhill trap that involved lies and deceptions. The problem with these foundations is that they constantly need more of the same to survive. Once a lie is told, another takes its place just as quickly. He also had the added label of "stupid" to overcome from his stepfather, and he was convinced that he had to prove that to be wrong. Having a child with a married woman fell into the stupid category, however, and did little to change his mindset. He wanted to be a good father to his son, but lacked the training. He could not draw from his own father who abandoned him. Life had dealt him a losing hand. Like in the game of poker, He knew that he could still come out on top with a solid bluff. He couldn't change the cards, but he could change how to play them. This time he chose to fold, and like his father, abandoned his son.

Joy was playing another game, much like Russian roulette. Cheating on her husband lost both her husband and the father of her child. She was thrown into the single parent role much like Jake's mother, except her situation was self-generated. Sin is like a single rotten apple in a bushel of good ones. If it is not removed, the entire bushel will become spoiled. Once the decision to break her vows was made, the bushel became infected.

Jake has been remorseful over abandoning his son to this day. He and Joy divorced and he did not see his son again. Watching him from across the courthouse atrium, I can still see the anguish in his heart. I know that he longs to see his son again who would now be about eighteen. Jake would like to say, *"I am so very sorry"* for leaving him. Yet, today, Jake is waiting for his day in court to rescue his two daughters from a second marriage. I have seen him with the children he now has with wife number three and fatherhood has done a complete turn around. His stepfather called him stupid and that is how he feels today regarding his first son. We don't get to turn back the clock and make amends very often. Somehow, I sit here and wonder if these things happened for a reason. I wonder if everything was part of a script with the final scene about to unfold.

THE JUDGE

Once again, Jake sought a life of deceit. He could not return home to his parents, and his only friends were gang members. Aaron had also moved out and found a place of his own. It was a small apartment, but Jake was welcome to crash there, at least until he could get back on his feet. He knew how to roof and contracted some jobs under the table, which gave him some reprieve from selling dope. He never finished high school, but seemed to readily pick up any activity that used his hands. Roofing also added a sense of thrill as he would take on difficult highly pitched roofs. He appeared fearless as he tackled these jobs. It was as if he had claws in his footwear that gripped the surface without fear of falling. The quality of his work was recognized by each customer who, readily, recommended him to others needing roof repairs.

Aaron had taken back his father's knife and luger before leaving the family home. The gun traveled with him on a regular basis as he worked in a high crime area of the city. Occasionally, thugs would meet him to demand money, and the gun quickly became his equalizer. On one occasion, Jake went with Dawg to the bank to make a deposit, when he realized that the luger was on his possession. He thought that the security inside the bank might have some form of weapon sensing, so he handed the gun to Jake. Jake placed the gun behind his shirt and against his lower back, as he had done so often in his room during his pretend sessions. When Dawg returned, the only thing on his mind was to get to work. He dropped Jake off to be with his friends in the "Orange Crush" and sped away. The luger was still cold against Jake's back.

The events of that day were like something out of a Hollywood script. Nothing good was to come from a gang of hoodlums out for a good time, with one of them packing heat. The gang might not have started out looking for trouble that day, but it found them, nonetheless. Alcohol and a few joints had already warped each gang member's senses, when they spotted some would-be tourists as targets for petty theft to further enhance their habits. What they did not realize was their preys were off duty police with their families on vacation. Although, the Orange Crush quickly dispersed, Jake was apprehended. The luger was spotted and Jake became a suspect even before the gang had a chance to establish their cause.

Carrying a weapon without a permit was a crime. This time Jake did not talk his way out of doing time. After a week in the local lock- up, he was brought before a judge. He was charged with one count of weapon possession and two counts of drug possession, having two "bags" in his pocket. He was now over the age of eighteen and was responsible for his own actions. Even if Joe desired to bail him out once again, the courts would not allow it. The gun may have belonged to Aaron, but not under the law. It was unregistered. Aaron might have remembered to ask for it back after leaving the bank, but he didn't. The whole day was like a bad dream as he replayed it in his mind.

> *"All rise. The court is now in session. The honorable Judge Carter presides."*

These were the first words that Jake heard in that courtroom. Judge Carter proceeded to walk slowly up the stairs behind the cherry stain colored bench that seemed to be ten feet tall (although the top was more like five feet). Jake stood up with his hands cuffed in front. His hair was neatly combed, and he was wearing a clean jail cell uniform. After Judge Carter sat down, he motioned for the audience to sit, including Jake.

The judge looked down through his narrow reading glasses to read the long history of petty crimes, misdemeanors, and possession charges of the past. Occasionally, he would look up over his glasses at Jake who stood before him. To Jake, the look was one of concern more than disgust. He had not seen such a glance and did not know how to interpret it. All he knew was this was the "Judge." His friends often had made comments about going before the "Judge" for various crimes. Each time the results were not very desirable. Being in front of the judge solicited a fear that did not bring on the euphoric high that he expected.

Somehow, the judge represented an authority beyond anything he had known before. He was, somehow, bigger than life. He knew that he could not strike any measure of fear into the judge, especially with his hands cuffed together and several armed guards in the courtroom.

After several minutes of standing, Judge Carter once again looked up over his spectacles. His eyes pierced Jake's mind and heart as if to say, *"Son, you are in a whole lot of trouble."* It was a look that Jake found difficult to explain, and one he wouldn't forget anytime soon. The judge leaned over his bench and asked:

> *"How has your accommodations been, Mr. Jake?" (He was referring to the jail cell.)*

Jake was taken by surprise by his question, and answered,

> *"Fine, sir."*

Judge Carter did not respond immediately, causing Jake some additional time to ponder what would come next. The wait, although only a few seconds, seemed like eternity. Then the judge asked:

> *"Where did you get the gun son?"*

Jake knew that he could not let the judge know that Aaron was carrying it that day, so he answered:

> *"From my father's World War II collection."*

Judge Carter knew from the transcripts that Jake's father was a retired military man, but also knew that his service time began long after WWII had ended. The Korean War was also fought before his father enlisted. Again, the judge paused to allow Jake some time to think about his answer. Then he looked at him and said:

> *"Your dad has a wonderful military background, but not during that war son. So where did you get the gun?"*

Jake might have thought that his first answer would satisfy the judge's question, but was now faced with a new dilemma. He had to tell the truth without implicating his brother. He answered the judge with the words:

> *"The gun belonged to my brother's father. Actually, he is my adopted brother as both his parents died and we took him in. His father was drafted as a teenager during the war. The gun was my brother's keepsake from his dad."*
> *"Is your brother, Aaron?"* the judge responded.
> *"Yes."*
> *"Did he give you the gun?"*

Jake was once again feeling trapped by his response. He remembers the first time Dawg showed him the luger. He asked him to store it so that mom would not find it while renovating his bedroom. He recalled the shoebox that held the weapon. So Jake answered:

> *"Sir, my brother kept it in a shoebox and I knew where he kept it. I was approached by a gang the week before and decided to take it with me for protection."*

Again the judge used the power of silence to allow Jake to reflect upon his answer. Aaron had a few run-ins with the law, but his criminal record appeared trivial in comparison to Jake's. The judge looked down through his glasses as if he was reading, but then looked up again to capture his demeanor. If Jake were lying, he would sense it. His years of judicial experience taught him some of the telltale signs to look for like twitching, nervousness, or sweating. None of these were evident. Jake was focused on the day he first saw the gun and the partial truth. The events of that morning were lost for the moment. The judge changed the questioning.

> *"So, did you intend to use the gun, son?"*
> *"I hope not, sir. I just did not want to feel intimidated again."*
> *"If you were intimidated, would you have used it?"*
> *"I don't think I would fire it, sir, but I might have pulled it out to get them to back off."*
> *"I see. So you don't desire a fight, but you won't back down either. Is that right?"*
> *"Yes, sir."*

The conviction in Jake's voice was both admirable and disturbing. It is one thing to stand up for yourself and quite another to rely on a weapon as an equalizer. The judge felt it to be in Jake's best interest and society's to place him in confinement. As an adult this meant federal prison and he would be permanently scarred with the label, "felon." Then there was the question of "how long?" Jake could have been given up to five years. Thirty days would be too short. After some deliberation, the judge looked back at Jake and said:

> *"Son, your record of misdemeanors has demonstrated that you have not learned from past mistakes. You are a threat to society and yourself, especially when you carry a loaded weapon, whether intending to use it or not. I understand that your father left very early in your life and that you are burning a torch against him. I see boys like you come and go in my courtroom rather routinely, and the one piece of common ground is a lack of fatherly discipline. Therefore, I am sentencing you to four months in a federal prison. This sentence is light, as you know I could have sent you away for years. I desire that you find a way to release the hatred you have for your father and authority in general. I see potential in you that right now you do not see in yourself. Do you have anything to say for yourself?"*

Jake appeared somewhat stunned. He was going to the "Big House," and yet felt something calm him inside. The words, "I see potential in you" were a far cry from "you are stupid," which his stepfather uttered. It was as if these words were exactly what he needed to hear. Someone actually cared about him. Four months did not sound too bad as he expected a sentence much harsher. Throughout the communication in that courtroom, he also recalled several times when the judge referred to Jake as "Son." That image penetrated his mind. He responded with the words, *"No sir."*

The judge removed his glasses and laid them on the bench. He then motioned for Jake to step towards him. He readily responded without incident. It may have been the first time in his adult life that he acted respectfully towards anyone in authority. He might not have known what the judge was about to say, but he was willing to listen. Perhaps, the father that he never knew was wearing a judicial robe that day, and he wanted to lean on him. Each time the judge referred to Jake as "Son," may have pierced his heart. In any event, he humbly moved to hear what the judge was about to say.

> *"Come up close to the bench, Son. What I have to share is now for your ears only."*

Jake responded. Then Judge Carter leaned over the bench and lovingly peered into Jake's eyes. Then he said, softly:

> *"Son. I want you to know that I have empathy for you. Do you know what the word empathy means?*

After a brief pause, Jake responded, *"No sir."*

> *"Empathy is like being inside your shoes and understanding what you are going through. Let me explain. I lost my father in the Korean War. I was about seven at the time, not much older than you were when your father left. I held anger inside for many years. I even blamed myself in part for his death. I rationalized that my father was more worried about me here in the states, then the war in front of him. If he was more focused on the battle than me, he may still be alive. Does that sound odd to you, son?"*
>
> *"No sir. I have felt some guilt over my dad leaving as well."*
>
> *"You're feelings are quite common, son. The hundreds of divorce proceedings, involving children that I have overseen, have siblings emotionally scarred with those same feelings. Before I have my bailiff escort you out of this courtroom, I want you to know some things from someone who has some understanding of what you are going through. I desire that you know more about the man you can be, than the one you know at this moment. You are about to enter a world, unlike anything you have known before. You can choose to respect the authority and learn from the experience, or you can take a different path. I want you to choose wisely. I believe in you.*

After a pause, he looked down for a brief moment, and then looked up at the judge. The judge saw a tear drip down the side of his face. Words did not have to be spoken, but Jake asked, *"Sir, did you ever release the anger and guilt that you had toward your father?"*

"I did, son. I did, but not until I became a father, myself. I was not angry with my father. I was angry with God for taking him from me. When I had a family of my own, I realized that I needed my heavenly father to help me be the best parent and husband that I could be. I know that, as men, we are mere mortals with flaws. My Christian pride helped me to see that. I recommitted my life to serving Christ. Do you know Him, son?"

"I use His name a lot, but I do not know Him."

"My wife gave me some verses to help me know Jesus. I will make sure that you have them noted in a Bible that I will personally give to you. Read it daily during your incarceration. The verses are:

Ephesians 2:10 (NIV)

For we are God's workmanship, created in Christ Jesus to do good works, which God prepared in advance for us to do.

These words helped me to understand that I may have come from earthly parents, but that God, through His Son, Jesus Christ, had something better planned.

Romans 15: 4 (NIV)

"For everything that was written in the past was written to teach us, so that through endurance and the encouragement of the scriptures we might have hope."

Reading the Bible daily not only gave me hope, but also became my hope. The words became real and alive.

Philippians 4: 10-13 (NIV)

[10] I rejoiced greatly in the Lord that at last you renewed your concern for me. Indeed, you were concerned, but you had no opportunity to show it.

¹¹ I am not saying this because I am in need, for I have learned to be content whatever the circumstances.
¹² I know what it is to be in need, and I know what it is to have plenty. I have learned the secret of being content in any and every situation, whether well fed or hungry, whether living in plenty or in want.
¹³ I can do all this through him who gives me strength.

I knew that I had to let go of myself and let God have the reins of control in my life. I let Him be my strength.

John 3" 16 – 21 (NIV)

¹⁶ For God so loved the world that he gave his one and only Son, that whoever believes in him shall not perish but have eternal life.
¹⁷ For God did not send his Son into the world to condemn the world, but to save the world through him.
¹⁸ Whoever believes in him is not condemned, but whoever does not believe stands condemned already because they have not believed in the name of God's one and only Son.
¹⁹ This is the verdict: Light has come into the world, but people loved darkness instead of light because their deeds were evil.
²⁰ All those who do evil hate the light, and will not come into the light for fear that their deeds will be exposed.
²¹ But those who live by the truth come into the light, so that it may be seen plainly that what they have done has been done in the sight of God.

I knew there was a right way and a wrong way to live in this world, but I could not see the path. I realized that I needed a guiding light. I also began to believe that if we are here for a purpose, then there must be something after we die or our efforts will be in vain. I began to actually feel God's love upon me in a way that I could only dream about from my earthly father.

Romans 6:23 (NIV)

For the wages of sin is death, but the gift of God is eternal life in Christ Jesus our Lord.

I began to understand what sin is. Although I did not rebel to the point of coming before a judge, I realized that I needed Jesus to forgive me for everything and anything that kept me from a right relationship with my heavenly father.

> *"Jake, these words may not mean a lot to you today, but I want you to know that someone cares about you and all that you can accomplish. Your future begins with the steps you take from this day forward. You may not understand what I am about to tell you now, but it is my sincere hope that you will someday. I will be praying for you every day of your confinement. I truly believe that you are here before me today for a higher purpose than either of us understands right now. I hope you find out what that is."*

The barrage of scripture that was just thrown at him took Jake a step back. He came to hear his sentence and received a sermon. Yet, there was something in the eyes of Judge Carter that stirred his heart. He stood there listening and all the while felt a calmness that he had not felt before. He entered the courtroom that morning with apprehension. Somehow, that anxiety was gone. The four-month sentence was far less than he had anticipated. As the bailiff escorted him to the holding area for further instructions, he had a feeling of relief. Perhaps, it was because Dawg was not implicated. Jake would reflect upon this moment throughout his confinement.

The judge said that he would be praying for Jake every day of his prison term. The concept of prayer was somewhat foreign to Jake. There might have been a time in his young life when circumstances caused him to cry out *"Oh God!"* But, for the most part, talking to someone that you cannot see sounded ludicrous, like having a make-believe friend. He listened intently to everything that the judge spoke, but he could not understand what prayer was all about or its impact. Yet, there was something in those words that came across so sincere, that he felt a form of relief. He understood that prayer meant something to the judge. The fact that the judge cared enough to talk to his God about Jake offered solace.

Then the question of purpose came to mind. Judge Carter mentioned that he felt things happen for a reason. He believed that it was no coincidence that Jake was in his courtroom that day. Somehow, it was all part of an overarching plan. Jake pondered this idea in his heart. Each time he gave his thoughts a voice, the same questions would come out.

"Why did dad walk out?"
"What purpose would that have for my life?"
"Why did mom have to remarry?"
"What was our time in Hawaii all about?"
"Why Virginia and the River Rats?"
"Why did Dawg spare me from a thrashing?"
"Why did he lose his parents?"
"Why did he come to live with us?"

The why questions had few answers. Yet, there was something compelling in Judge Carter's words. He believed that Jake had a date with destiny in his courtroom, orchestrated by a higher power. Jake might not have believed those words were true, but he respected the judge. Perhaps, time will bring answers.

INCARCERATION

The holding area included several other felons awaiting transportation to the prison, which was about thirty miles away. Jake was told to sit, and a court-assigned guard kept vigil. Although he remained silent, most of the detainees were vocally claiming injustices and using the name of God irreverently. One young man, directly across from Jake, was quietly sitting with his head shamefully bowed. Jake was drawn to the man and watched intently. He was burly and appeared to be in his late twenties. Physically, the man had several tattoos and looked like he could hold his own in a street fight. Jake was so fixated on him that he could hardly hear the loud clamor in the room from the rest of the prisoners.

The bus arrived a few hours later and the men were aligned in single file to get on the bus. There were twelve men in all. Each man was given a separate assigned seat next to the windows, with their arms and legs chained to the floor. A man in uniform stood at the driver's area and gave instructions after every prisoner was seated. They were not to speak unless spoken to directly. Jake sat across from the man who held his attention in the holding room. He wanted to start a conversation with him, but thought better of it after the announcements were made. The thirty-mile trek took approximately forty-five minutes.

The bus pulled into the prison and two sets of barb-wired gates closed behind. Reality struck. This would be Jake's home for the next four months. He did not know how long the rest of the men would be there, but was curious about the quiet burly man's fate. One by one they were released from the chains that held them captive to the bus and were escorted to another holding area inside the prison. Armed guards were posted, seemingly everywhere. After the men were assembled, a man wearing a suit was escorted to the room by three armed guards.

> *"My name is Warden Jackson. While you are here, I am your father, your boss, and your lord. You will answer me with the word "Sir." Your stay under my control can be marked with difficulty or with a measure of relief, but the choice is yours alone. All authority is mine. Is that understood?*
> "Sir, yes sir." Was the response from only a few, Jake included.
> *"I CAN'T HEAR YOU."*
> This time the entire group responded: "SIR, YES SIR."

Jake knew immediately what it would take to make his stay as easy as possible. The authority in the warden's voice demanded respect and humility. Warden Jackson was like a drill sergeant, and Jake was now in basic training. This was a stark contrast from what he was used to. He controlled the strings of his mother and stepfather. Now he was the one being controlled. He also remembered the words of Judge Carter only a few hours earlier. Jake did not fully grasp the significance of those words, but knew that endurance came from hope, and that hope came from a place outside of his control. When the warden spoke, he listened intently, and responded with respect.

After receiving the customary scrub downs, wardrobes, and various other toiletry items, the men were escorted to their narrow cells, two per room. Jake was initially paired with a very vocal tall man, but at the last moment moved to the same cell as the burly man who sat quietly in the court's holding area. Seeing the man, who he wanted to start a dialog on the bus, seemed to offer a small light in the dismal circumstance. The cell doors slammed with a loud bang and then a clang, indicating that the lock was secured.

> *"What's your name?* Jake asked his new roommate.
> *"John White. What's yours?" "Jake."*
> *"Just Jake? Do you have a last name?"*
> *"It's Wilson, but I have not heard anyone call me anything but Jake."*
> *"Jake it is then. You can call me Johnny."*

"Johnny, how long are you in for? This was one of the questions that Jake wanted to ask on the bus ride to the prison.

"Six months. What about you?"

"Four months for me. I thought sure it would be a lot longer with my history. They got me for packin' and drugs. What about you?"

"Abuse. I was up for attempted murder as I came close to killing someone."

"It sounds like you got off light as well."

"Yeah! If the police had not arrived when they did, it would have been murder. I was in a rage."

"What did he do?"

"He hit a neighbor lady outside my apartment complex. I was getting out of my car when I heard them yelling. They were near the front entrance of the complex. She couldn't have weighed a hundred pounds, and he was huge. She must have said the wrong thing as I saw him hit her across the face with a blow that sent her reeling over a handrail and into some bushes. Something snapped inside me. I ran towards the man and started wailing. It took him by surprise as he hardly got a lick in."

"If I saw that, I would have done the same thing. I don't let people push me around, but hitting a woman is despicable."

"Yeah! When I see that, I snap. My dad used to beat my mom when I was young. I heard her crying and I wished it would stop."

"Where's your dad now, Johnny?"

"I don't know. They divorced before I started high school. The last time I heard from him was in a card when I graduated. It was postmarked Oregon, but that was ten years ago."

"Where's your mother?"

"She lives less than an hour's ride from the prison. You may meet her during a visit, at least I hope we can have visitors."

"Me too. My mom and stepdad don't live that far away, either."

"So Jake, what's your story?"

Jake began to tell his story and the two of them seemed to bond. It was as if they were brought together to that place for a higher purpose. Both men had fatherly issues that haunted them, although quite different circumstances. Judge Carter's words made a permanent imprint in Jake's mind. Somehow, the events of Jake's life had led him to this small cell at this particular time in his life.

Suddenly, a loud siren blasted and additional guards appeared on the cell wing. The cell doors were unlocked and the prisoners were directed to the prison yard. The twelve new guests stood before Warden Jackson to receive directions for their stay.

"Welcome to your new home."

The words may have triggered different thoughts to each man standing there, but Jake had a completely different picture of what "home" was. Video games, television and tape players were now missing from his new reality.

"You men will eat when I tell you to eat. You will sleep when I say sleep. You will earn privileges. Until your stay is over, your life is what I say it is. Do you understand?'
"Sir, yes sir." The response may not have sounded sincere, but it was unanimous. Jake wondered if TV and video games were an earned privilege.

The indoctrination lasted about thirty minutes. The next four months were now laid out in a structure; unfamiliar to anything Jake had known before. Breakfast was at six. Work detail started at six forty- five. Lunch was at noon, and supper at six. Lights out at nine and the new day repeated the sequence, except for Sunday. Sunday was a day of rest, at least from the work detail part. The warden made it clear, however, that strict adherence to the rules during the week was required to enjoy that day of rest. Time was also available for physical exercise and strength training.

In addition, a prison library was available. Reading was not one of Jake's strong points. He did not graduate from high school and anything that did not involve using his hands was not well received. Even though writing was a hand exercise, it involved spelling, which Jake had a very limited vocabulary. Jake remembered Judge Carter's words about receiving a Bible with the words he quoted marked. He remembered the many Bibles at his grandfather's home, which he would read on occasion to Jake when he visited. If he was able to visit a library in the prison and opened a Bible, these words would not be easily located. Yet, he believed the judge and waited anxiously for the marked-up gift.

Prison life had its obstacles to be sure, but for Jake, there was solace. He had found a measure of peace and made a new friend. He kept his nose clean, though the pressures from other inmates caused him to take a stand from time to time. He earned their respect, much like he did in his gangs. Incarceration was also a defining time in his life. A month before his release, he found an inmate, skilled in tattoo artistry. A ball and chain was tattooed onto his right ankle as a reminder and a status symbol. Anyone in the yard who saw it knew that he earned respect.

THE VISIT

During the warden's opening remarks in the yard, visitation and mail was discussed. Felons could write to anyone they wanted, but all letters would be screened through the warden before mailing. Inappropriate words would either be removed (blackened out) or the letter would be returned to the writer with a warning. Jake thought about sending a letter to Aaron, but calling him "Dawg" might fit into that inappropriate category.

Visitation was limited to a three-hour window sandwiched around lunchtime. Visitors would be properly screened, almost as if they were felons, and visits would be held to fifteen minutes or less. There would be no physical contact. Plexiglas panels allowed visitors and felons to see one another, but phone devices served for audio communication. Any potential gifts needed to be passed through the warden's assigned services, including home baked cookies and cakes. The warden's staff did not appear lacking in calorie intake, so there may have been taste testing as part of their vocation.

Mail call came each day at three in the afternoon, when the convicts had a moment of rest from their work. Work details were not like splitting rocks with pick axes, as seen in the Hollywood movies. Convicts were given a list of tasks they could perform, which produced some benefit to the prison establishment. The warden had prisoners tested for their unique abilities, and he assigned the work details accordingly. Jake's aptitude clearly involved some form of construction using his hands. His assignments included brick laying, roofing, and some plumbing, which came in handy, as each cell was equipped with a small sink and toilet.

Johnny worked in the prison mess hall as a dishwasher. The two men would discuss their workday each night in their cell. After the discussion,

Jake felt a great sense of relief. At least his work was different on a daily basis. One day he might fix a roof. On another day, he might lay bricks or replace faucet o-rings. He did not need a book of instructions as each task came natural. There was also a sense of satisfaction at the end of each work session, as Jake could look back and see what he accomplished. Johnny did not complain, however.

The nightly discussion helped to create a bond between them, along with several moments of laughter, like the time Jake had to repair a clogged sink in one of the cells. Usually, Jake would remove the trap below the sink's basin and find it full of hair. That was the case this day.

> *"Johnny. I had to clean out a basin at the end of our block. It was so full of hair that you almost needed a drill to get through it."*
> *"Whose cell was it?"*
> *"Mac's."*
> *"You mean the Jordan brothers?"*
> *"I don't think that they are brothers, except they are both black men."*

Johnny started laughing hysterically. In the short time they were incarcerated, nicknames were handed out routinely. Mac and his cellmate were bald black men resembling the superstar basketball player, Michael Jordan. The label, "Jordan Brothers," fit their physical appearance. Jake began to chuckle because of Johnny's inability to stop.

> *"Do you think they came here with a full head of hair?"*
> Johnny said while trying to stop laughing.
> *"Maybe,"* Jake snickered. *"But, the hair was mostly blonde."*

The two men began to laugh so uncontrollably, that the rest of the cellblock joined in. Even the guards on duty found it difficult to hold back the tears. The laughter was contagious and a welcomed relief for the men there. The guards also welcomed moments of humor. The sounds of vulgarity and moaning were the normal on their watch. Even after the lights went out, a snicker or chuckle would send a new wave of hilarity throughout the ward. Anytime the name, Michael Jordan, was uttered, the scene would repeat. It was times like these that helped Jake cope with the time spent behind the cold steel bars of his cell.

Visitation times also helped spell relief. Jake had been in prison for two weeks, when he received his first visitor.

"Jake. You have a visitor."

These words came directly from the warden after Jake had finished eating his noontime meal. Jake wondered if his mother had made the trip up to see him. He had received a few letters from her, but there was no mention of any visit in the immediate future. As he was escorted to the holding room, behind the Plexiglas panels, thoughts began to stream through Jake's mind. If it was not his mother, then it must be Dawg. But, Aaron had not contacted him at all during his stay. Perhaps, Dawg came as a surprise? The walk to the room was somewhat invigorating in anticipation.

The door to the room was unlocked and the guard entered with Jake. Except for the guard standing near the door, Jake was alone. He peered through the clear panel in front of the assigned seat that he was told to take. He was given instructions on how to use the headphones and the talk button in the center of the shelf in front of him. There was no one on the other side. Thoughts kept racing through his mind. Someone wanted to see him, and he could not wait until he saw who it was.

The door to the guest area slowly opened. Behind the guard entering was a man wearing a long trench coat and hat. He certainly was not any member of Jake's family based on his appearance. The door was partially obscured from Jake's vision, but then he saw his face. Judge Carter had made a personal trip just to see Jake. He placed his hat and coat on a table near the entrance and then reached in the coat pocket for something. Jake could not see what the object was, and was wondering why the judge came to visit him.

The judge was directed to Jake's window and he sat down. He smiled at Jake and started to speak, but the words were not heard on Jake's side of the Plexiglas. Then Judge Carter picked up the receiver hanging on a clip on the side of the window.

"How are things with you Jake? Are you getting settled in?"

"Things are going well, Judge. What brings you here to see me?"
"Don't you remember my promise Jake?"
"What promise?"
"I told you that I would mark up a Bible and get it to you. I thought at the time that I would get it to the warden, but I decided to deliver it personally."
"I remember, Judge. They have a small room full of books that they call a library in this place. I don't read much, but I kept looking for a Bible there. Trouble is, when I find one the verses that I wanted to read are mixed among thousands of pages."
"Yeah! I know what you mean, Jake. The first time I tried to pick up the Bible just to read, I found myself getting lost and confused."
"Its not even in English," Jake replied, referring to the King James Version that he had opened in the prison library.
"What's 'Thou' anyway?" Judge Carter said with a sheepish grin on his face. *"But, then again, we say some strange things depending on where we are from, don't we Jake, like Yuns or Y'all? Our slang would be foreign to the old English people."*
"I never though of it that way, Judge."

Judge Carter was already impressed with the progress Jake was making during incarceration. Each time Jake responded, there was a noticeable element of respect in his voice. He could also see a sense of real joy in his face, unlike the man who stood before him in his courtroom a few weeks earlier. Then Judge Carter placed the Bible on the small shelf on his side of the Plexiglas. He began to open it to several pages that had colored tags attached. The scriptures, which he had shared with Jake in his courtroom, were highlighted in color.

"Jake. This is a more easily readable Bible for you called "The Living Bible." I figured the King James Version would be more difficult to understand. I have cleared it with the warden and the guard will make sure that you have it."

As Judge Carter handed the book to the guard, he could not help but notice a tear below Jake's right eye. The gift was received with love, a concept that may have been foreign to the man, whose father abandoned so early in his life.

> *"Why are you in tears?"*
> *"I can't believe that you did this for me, Judge. You honored your promise and even made it personal. You knew that I might have trouble with the old English, so you selected a Bible that I might be able to handle. You can't understand how that makes me feel."*
> *"I hope it makes you feel loved as well, Jake."*
> *"If love is a warm tingly feelin', then I guess I feel it."*

The visit was a new defining moment for both Jake and Judge Carter. Never before had the judge seen such emotion in one of his sentenced felons, especially in such a short time. It was a moment that would bring more visits between the two men. With each new meeting, Judge Carter would bring a few more verses for Jake to study. It made his chosen profession as a judge more meaningful than ever before. Jake was now much more than a lawbreaker. He was but a lump of coal, but to the judge, he was a diamond in the making. He saw Jake's potential and wanted him to also find it for himself.

> *"So what have they got you doing, Jake?"*
> *"I guess they found out that I like to use my hands, so they have me roofing, brick laying, and fixing the plumbing around this place. I enjoy it, but don't tell anyone. They may change my work to something else. Prison isn't supposed to be fun is it?"*
> *"It is if you choose to make it that way, Jake. You are here to find yourself, and that involves a lot of choices. The warden has shared with me that you are keeping up your end in this place."*

The concept of making choices was relatively new to Jake. As he began to look back on his life, he could see that he had been making many choices all along, like joining each gang or dropping out of school. He had not yet understood that he made choices when his father left. The anger and pain, felt as a five-year old boy, was directly linked to his father. To Jake that was not a choice. The words from the judge would have a profound impact in Jake's life as the two men began to bond.

When Judge Carter shared that the warden had a good report, Jake felt something else inside. He was in contact with the warden every day, but he could only venture a guess as to what the warden thought about him. The judge's words were a comfort. They gave Jake a new sense of respect for the warden.

> *"So Jake, how's Johnny doing?"*
> *"You know Johnny?"* Jake responded with a look of curiosity.
> *"I know him. You and Johnny are a lot alike. That's why I asked the warden to place you together in the same cell."*

Jake was somewhat taken back by his words. He recalled the events of that day, when Johnny was assigned to his cell. At the time, Jake thought it was strange, as the tall boisterous man was first assigned. Just as quickly, Johnny was told to take his place instead. Now, Jake learned that Judge Carter was the one who was involved in that decision. He had wondered, briefly, about the incident that first day, but was grateful to get Johnny as a cellmate.

> *"Johnny has been a great friend in here. Thank you for helping to get him as my roomy."*
> *"My pleasure, Jake. Has he talked about his life with you?"*
> *"He said that he had a temper, which landed him here."*
> *"He almost killed a man. In my opinion, the man deserved the beating."*
> *"So why did you send Johnny up, Judge?"*
> *"Johnny is a loose cannon. If I had let him go, he would have been back in my courtroom within a week. Besides, I had to act on the law. The woman that was struck claimed that it was an accident."*
> *"Accident my foot. He beat her. Johnny saw it and said it was no accident. He was in a rage."*
> *"I believe you, Jake. She is his wife and refused to press charges against him. I can tell you from experience that she had felt his wrath many times before."*
> *"If I was there, judge, he would have felt my wrath. You just don't go around hitting women."*

"Unfortunately, Jake, this scenario is all too common. Its bad enough to see people under the influence of alcohol or drugs commit cruel acts, but many husbands feel that they have a right to beat their wives. Often the wives are too scared to stand up and do what is right to stop the abuse. They even try to justify it as their fault."

"I was married, Judge, but I never thought like that."

"I am not saying that all men feel that way. With the anger you have harbored against your father, you could have used it against your wife, but you didn't. There's some good in you."

The two smiled and then broke out in laughter. It was not because of the words spoken, but the attitude behind the words. Judge Carter had touched a soft spot in Jake's heart. Whenever, he spoke about the future and offered a wry grin, Jake understood that the judge cared, and would return the gesture. In his courtroom Judge Carter spoke with great authority, but Jake pictured the stares over the man's reading glasses. He recalled the moments of silence before Judge Carter spoke, and could see the caring eyes behind the words. Jake thought about both looks at length for his entire stay in the prison.

"Try and get Johnny to open up with you, Jake. It will do both of you a world of good. I think he is a good reader as well, so if you need help with the words in your new Bible, he can help."

"You got me interested in learning more about Johnny. I will see what I can do."

"That's good. I see my time is up, so I must go now."

"Will you come back again, Judge?"

"I will when I can. My caseload severely limits my availability, however. It has been a pleasure sharing with you, Jake. I hope you read the scriptures that I outlined, daily."

"I will try."

"You will Jake. I hate the word 'try.' It should be taken out of the English language. People tell me that they will try and be there, but never show. It is an excuse. When they don't show up they say, "Well at least I tried."

"I never thought about that, Judge. I say it all the time. I will read from the book when I can. I can't promise that it will be

*every day, but when the lights are on in my cell and I am there,
I will read."*
"You do that, Jake, and you will not be sorry. Trust me."

For the first time Jake realized something about what it meant to trust someone. Judge Carter kept his promise and earned his trust. He said he would deliver a Bible and he did. No one else had made the trip down to visit him, not even his family. Judge Carter made an impression on an eighteen year-old man by following up on his promise. Jake knew something about keeping commitments with his gang mentality, but there was something deeper with the judge. He not only cared about Jake, but also about Johnny. Jake wondered what this day was all about. Was it about a man delivering on a promise? Or, was it far more than that?

THE YARD

Jake returned to the yard after his visit with the judge. It almost seemed like a dream. He gave himself a pinch to see if it was real. The guard took the new Bible to Jake's cell for safekeeping. He assured him that it would be tucked beneath his pillow on the upper bunk in his cell.

The prison held many first time offenders, but also was home to a few long-term felons. These were kept in an isolated area without the privilege of a work release program to allow them to develop skills, which can be used upon release. Anger, resentment, and other negative feelings were present in both groups, but short-term prisoners could earn the right to apply themselves. Although, they would need to learn respect for authority as part of their stay, they were also given opportunities to find a niche in society on release. The hope is that they will not return.

Johnny had been waiting in the yard, anxiously anticipating his return. Jake was so caught up in the moment that he did not see Johnny running towards him shouting:

> *"Who was it, Jake? Who was it?"*
> *"Hi Johnny."* Jake still had not heard what Johnny was saying, but caught him out of the corner of his eye.
> *"So, are you going to tell me who your visitor was, Jake? Was it you mom or your brother?"*
> *"No. It was the judge who sentenced me. You know him, too."*
> *"Judge Carter?" "Yeah!"*
> *"He handed down my sentence. I liked him, however." "Yeah! Me, too! He's okay."*

"So what did he want? Why did he select you, Jake?"
"Remember when I told you that he was going to mark up a Bible and get it to me here in this place?"
"I remember, Jake."
"Well, he brought it to me today."
"So, where is it?"
"I had the guard take it back to my cell. I did not want to get it ruined in the yard or while I worked."
"Wow! I can't believe that he brought it personally, Jake. He must see some good in you." Johnny said this with a hint of cynicism in his voice.
"He likes you too, Johnny."
"Did he say that, Jake?"
"Yeah! He also said that he talked to the warden to have us as roomies."
"He really said that, huh?"
"He said that we are cut from the same mold, well, sort of."
"I can't believe it. You mean that we are together in this place, because a judge thought it would be a good thing?"

Once again, Johnny's face wore a sheepish grin, soliciting a similar reaction from Jake.

"Who'd have thunk, huh?"
"So what did you two talk about? You were gone a long time."
"It seemed like only a few seconds. He shared some things about both of us. He said that he saw something in me that deserved a personal visit."
"What could he possibly see in you, Jake? Maybe, he wants a new roof when you get out."

The two men smiled and parted for their assigned duties. The discussion would resume later in their cell. They did not get to have meals very often together, due to Johnny's job in the kitchen. The brief time between lunch and Jake's work was another moment. Jake thought it somewhat odd that he would return from his first visitation at that particular time. Normally, Johnny would have been preparing for the evening meal, but the first person to greet him after the visit was Johnny. It was as if everything was preplanned. Jake would dwell on this coincidence throughout the rest of the day.

The visit from Judge Carter that day was another defining moment for Jake. No one had ever demonstrated such concern for Jake; not his mother, not his stepfather, and especially not his father. Judge Carter only knew him for less than an hour in his courtroom, and felt compelled to provide a follow up personal visit. He followed through on his promise to provide Jake with a Bible. The whole scene seemed like a dream, and he did not want to wake up. The rest of the day's activities were pale in comparison.

Even the yard appeared different, each time Jake returned. He could picture Johnny running towards him as soon as he returned from the visit. Not only did the judge care about him, but also so did Johnny. Knowing that the two men were celled together, because of the judge's influence, did wonders for both men. Jake and Johnny became the best of friends that day. They now had something in common. Judge Carter showed compassion, and both men felt it.

At the end of the day, Jake returned to his cell and found the Bible under his pillow as the guard had said. He began to read the verses highlighted. A short time later, Johnny returned and asked Jake to read aloud.

> *"I am not the best reader, Johnny."*
> *"That's OK. I still want to hear."*

Jake began to read from Romans 15:4.

> *"These things that were written in the Scrip..."* Jake paused with a look of confusion.
> *"That's Scriptures, Jake."*
> *"I remember Judge Carter using that word, but I am not sure what it meant."*
> *"Scriptures refer to words in the Bible, much like sentences are in a book."*
> *"These things that were written in the Scriptures so long ago are to teach us patience and to encourage us,"* Jake continued. *"If anyone needs encouragement, we do."*
> *"You got that right. We also need patience. Judge Carter wanted me to know that."*

> "I think he wanted me to understand that as well."
> "These words were not written just for us, Johnny. It says they were written a long time ago, so they must be for everybody."
> "If God is real, then it makes sense that He would provide instructions for us. Read on."
> "So that we will look forward expect…"
> "Let me see, Jake." Jake handed the Bible to Johnny who continued: "look forward expectantly to the time when God would conquer sin and death."
> "We will all die someday, Johnny. Does that mean that a time will come when people won't die?"
> "I guess so. What else could it mean? It also says that God will conquer sin. What does that mean?
> "I think sin is doing something wrong, like us. When you were before the judge, Johnny, didn't you know in your gut that you deserved your punishment?"
> "Yeah! What else did the judge mark up?"
> "He put colored tabs on each page. Turn to another one, Johnny."

Johnny flipped over to the yellow tab in Romans a few pages before the verse he just read. "For the wages of sin is death, but the free gift of God is eternal life through Jesus Christ our Lord."

> "There it is again, Johnny, sin and death. It seems to say that sin deserves death. We got off pretty light, don't you think?"
> "A few months sounds a whole lot better than dying. Did you catch the part about the free gift, Jake?"
> "You mean eternal life?"
> "Yeah! Doesn't that mean not dying?"
> "Eternity means forever, so I guess eternal life must mean being forever alive."
> "This is great stuff, Jake, great stuff. We need to dig deeper into this book."

Johnny flipped a page back and verse 5:3 seemed to leap out at him. "We can rejoice, too, when we run into problems and trials for we know that they are good for us – they help us to learn to be patient."

"If anyone in this world has problems and trials, Johnny, I'd say we are near the top of the list."

The two men pondered the words of scripture in their minds and hearts. They discussed each verse at length, but also gained insight from new verses. The process reinforced their patience and began to provide answers to many of their personal questions. It was as if the Bible was written especially for them. They could not wait to return to their cell to share about the day's events and have a time of Bible reading.

THE TEST

Nine o'clock would come all too quickly each evening. "Lights out" meant that the Bible needed to be closed. Yet, the discussion went on between the two cellmates for at least an hour afterwards. Scripture began to do just as it proclaimed, namely teach them patience. The men were model prisoners, as they did not want to lose the time they shared together. They were like brothers, except they did not fight. Each night, Jake would ask Johnny how his day went. After sharing, Johnny returned the question. Often, guards would hear them laughing, which was unique to the normal cell chatter.

Whenever Jake saw Johnny in the yard, the two would separate themselves and talk. Several of the other prisoners began to murmur amongst themselves.

"Do those two think they are better than us?" One would say.
"I hear them yakking long after the lights are out," Said another.
"I think they are Bible thumpers," Said a third.
"I'd like to teach them something about thumping."

Jake and Johnny did not hear the conversations, but could see the other convicts glaring at them. A few of these men were serving longer terms, but outside the yard time they were kept in confinement. Many were sentenced to a year or more. Jake's sentence was the lightest. The six-month tour for Johnny was also considered short term. Jake wondered if there was some jealousy brewing. Neither Jake, nor Johnny considered that the talk was about their biblical studying. As short- timers, they just wanted to do their time and leave the institution.

Three of the prisoners made their way over to where Jake and Johnny were seated. The biggest of the trio had a snake tattooed on his right arm, with the head positioned on the back of his hand. He seemed to be the spokesperson. When he pointed at Jake, the tattoo looked like a serpent about to strike.

> "So you think you are better than us, huh?"
> Jake stood and responded, "no."
> "You're no different than us, even if you only have a few months to serve. You're still criminals."
> Jake turned towards Johnny and asked, "What do you think?"
> "We're more than criminals, Jake. We're sinners."
> Jake nodded and looked back at the trio. "So, Snake, do you have a problem with Johnny and I wanting to be together?"
> "We feel, that if anyone has something to share, everyone needs to hear."
> "So is that why you guys gather in your small groups?

Jake had proven himself to his teenage friends as someone who would not back down from a confrontation, but this was a new venue. Snake and the rest of his associates had not met the test until now. Jake was bold in his approach and his words ignited a fire inside Snake.

> "Your name should be Jerk, not Jake."
> Jake responded with, "Maybe so, but Snake sure fits you. You are ready to strike your prey. Be careful. Sometimes the prey will strike back."
> "You think you're a mongoose?" (A mongoose is an animal that will attack a snake.)
> "Mongoose, huh? I never heard that one, but you don't know me very well. I don't back down from anyone, you included. Now if you want to know what Johnny and I are talking about as you claim, then I will tell you. We are discussing scripture."
> "So you're Bible thumpers?"
> "Not sure what that means, but if you want to study with us, you are all welcome to do so."

Snake wanted nothing to do with God. He lost a brother to cancer and a good friend to a drunk driver. If there was a God, then where was He in these situations?

"Come on guys. Let them have their time with their God."

The three men decided to leave without further incident. Jake remembered the moment well. He expected a confrontation and it did not happen, at least not with fists. Yet, there was something about that moment that was odd. He was ready for a fight. A part of him yearned for the rush that he used to feel in his gang brawls. The judge's Bible, which had captivated his thoughts, had become a dividing object between the rest of the convicts and the two cellmates. It seemed surreal. Without any hint of conflict, the men just turned and left by the mere mention of its name. The potential uprising was thwarted without any stand on Jake's part. He wondered, "Could it be that the God in the Bible was taking a stand for him that day?" Aaron stepped in to prevent a severe beating once, but this time there was no one, just the simple invitation to join in the Bible study. Somehow, that was all that was needed to cause the three men to turn around.

The rough looking men in the yard had quickly gotten the word to leave Johnny and Jake alone. The two men would be seen separated from the rest of the community of prisoners nearly every day, and no one bothered them. This was a scene that etched in Jake's mind for his prison stay. To him, prison was not the hard time that he originally thought it would be. The physical work was hard, but his temper held in check. It was like a step backwards in time. He could not shake the feeling that he was in that place for a reason, and that someone had his back.

THE LETTER

Except for extenuating circumstances, all prisoners were in their cells by eight P.M. Shortly after that, a guard walked by each cell carrying a small leather bag. Prisoners knew that time as the mail delivery. They would call the guard, "Mail boy." Long before the guard passed by Jake's cell he could hear chants.

> *"Hey Mail Boy. Anything in that sack for Jonesy."*
> *"You kidding? Who do you know who can write?"*
> *"A few packs of cigarettes don't need no writing."*
> *"Those things will kill you. Haven't you heard?"*
> *"You kill me, Mail Boy."*

When someone receives mail, everyone in the block knows about it by the verbal exchange. You could almost hear a pin drop as ears were facing outward along the entire cellblock. It was a time of anticipation, humor, and interaction between all of the prisoners.

> *"Hey Johnny. You got a letter today."*

The mail boy's words echoed throughout the cellblock. Johnny had not received any mail prior to that day, so his face appeared surprised. Jake was also caught up in the moment, as it was the first letter either man received. Curiosity got the best of both men.

> *"Maybe yo momma does care about you, Johnny boy,"* came from one cell.
> *"You got a girlfriend, Johnny? Make sure you tell her about all your friends in here,"* was another shout.

Mail time brought out nearly every sick thought or rough attempt at humor. In many ways, that time helped to draw the felons together. Both Jake and Johnny found themselves involved in the verbal rhetoric on earlier occasions. Jake enjoyed the exchange. It was like an escape from reality. Wit and humor marked a trail that would lead to more fun the next night. Sundays were a let down as no mail was delivered.

> The Mail Boy handed the letter to Johnny through the bars
> and said, *"First time, kid?"*
> *"Yeah."*
> *"The first one is always the most meaningful."*
> *"I hope so,"* replied Johnny.

Johnny took the letter and saw that the seal had been broken. He knew that all mail went through the warden's screening process before being distributed, so he wasn't upset. The sender's name was on the corner of the envelope, and it was not from family. The name was familiar, although Johnny could not put a face to it. The part that drew his attention, however, was the address. It was from the apartment complex, where he lived before his incarceration. He wondered if someone wanted money. If so, how could he pay from a prison cell? He thought of throwing the letter away without reading it.

> *"So, whose it from Johnny?"* began the chant.
> *"Yeah, tell us. We're dying out here."*
> *"Whataya staring at it for?"*

Johnny slowly removed the letter from the envelope. It was handwritten, but easy to read. It was too neat to be from a man. It was also short as only one side of the paper had text. Johnny began to read silently which further irked the other prisoners. Jake was too caught up in his friend's expressions to enter in the chant. After a minute or two, Johnny looked at his cellmate and said, *"I can't believe it, Jake. It's just not fair."*

> *"Believe what, Johnny?"* Jake responded.
> *"She's dead. It's not fair." "Whose dead?"*
> *"Yeah, whose dead, Johnny Boy?"* came from the cell next
> door.
> *"Maria. She's dead."*

"Maria? Whose she? Is she your girlfriend? Jake said with a hint of compassion.
"Maria. She's the reason I am in this place. I tried to help her. The man I beat up on shot her last night."

Jake asked to see the letter, and Johnny passed it to him. The look on Johnny's face seemed to say it all. He was serving time for nearly beating a man to death for striking Maria, and now that same man killed her. Life was not fair, at least at that moment. Jake took the letter, which read:

Dear Johnny,

I thought you should know that the woman you tried to help died last night a few minutes before midnight. Her apartment was so loud, that it woke me up, along with most of the other tenants. There was no shortage of swear words, mostly from her man. I heard two gunshots, but another neighbor heard three. Just as suddenly, the noise stopped.

The police were called before the shots were fired, due to the loud disturbance, but only arrived a few minutes later. George (Maria's husband) was taken away in cuffs. His tank top was smeared with blood. I hope they give him the chair. I told Maria to leave him many times, but she wouldn't. I think she feared him. Look what it got her anyway.

I wanted you to know, because I always felt that you got a bad rap. They should have taken George away that night and not you. Maybe if they did, Maria would still be alive.

Sincerely,

Sophie Bennett

Jake read the letter silently. The other felons were so vocal, that Jake also read it aloud for their ears. If he didn't the ward might not have slept much that night. The letter was a sharp reminder to both Jake and Johnny, that life was not fair. Though it was Johnny's rage that landed him in jail, his actions had a sense of merit. A woman could not defend herself, so Johnny stepped in to defend her. Now she was dead, less than two months later. No one said that life would be fair. Jake recalled similar feelings when his father left. Now he could only feel compassion for his friend.

"That was a good thing, Johnny, writing to you like that."

"I don't even know who she is, but I hope to meet her someday. Still, I am thankful for her."

"She really sounds sincere about you getting a bum rap and all, Johnny."

"I didn't think anyone cared."

"Sophie sure does. She took the time to write the letter and get a mailing address to get it to you."

"Yeah! I never thought that my first letter would come from a complete stranger."

"This sure is a strange place, Johnny. My first visitor was like that with Judge Carter."

"Sophie's address is on the envelope. Maybe, I can write back and thank her for being so considerate."

"You should Johnny. You should. What are you feeling right now?"

"Confused and maybe a bit angry. I can't help but think that I should have killed that man. Maria would still be alive."

"Yeah, but your life would be ruined. Things happen for a reason. I guess that is what we need to figure out, don't you think?"

"Perhaps, but Maria doesn't have that opportunity any more. Life sure is strange, Jake."

The two men had many conversations over the letter. Somehow, it marked a new direction in their nightly studies. Jake opened his Bible to a verse highlighted by the judge and began to read it several times. Ephesians 2:10 was the highlighted verse, but Jake began reading from the start of that section at verse eight.

[8] God saved you by his grace when you believed. And you can't take credit for this; it is a gift from God.

[9] Salvation is not a reward for the good things we have done, so none of us can boast about it.

[10] For we are God's masterpiece. He has created us anew in Christ Jesus, so we can do the good things he planned for us long ago.

"Johnny, do you believe that your life was planned? I mean when things happen to us, they are for a reason?"

"I dunno, Jake."
"If God does exist and cares about us, then it makes sense that He would provide some direction."
"So, do you think God had me beat up someone to help save his wife, only to learn that she died anyway by his hand?"
"I didn't say it makes sense, Johnny. Maybe, someday, we will understand. Still, you have to wonder, why things like this happen."
"I guess so, Jake."

The two men had deep theological questions surface after the letter arrived. Scripture reading began to take a new turn. Maria and Sophie became characters in their search to find the meaning of life. Johnny began to share from other events in his life, as did Jake. At times, they would stop and break out in uncontrollable laughter, usually, when both men had the same experience. One thing began to be quite evident, namely, they were meant to meet each other. To Jake, Johnny had become a brother. Judge Carter was right, when he told Jake that he and Johnny had a lot in common.

Slowly, the rage inside Johnny began to subside. He was more comfortable talking about his early childhood and watching his father beat on his mom. He used to talk about it and elevate his voice to almost a shout, but now he spoke calmly. "Why?" questions were still placed on the table, but somehow, the possible answers became less important. The idea, that someone might orchestrate anyone's life, began to take root. Jake recalled that day in Judge Carter's court when similar questions were raised.

Was Jake's life a jigsaw puzzle being slowly put together? Now Johnny was part of the mix. *"For we are God's masterpiece."* Those words seemed to indicate that our life is like a canvas, and God is placing His brush strokes as He pleases for the final work of art. Any portrayal of life in prison as some form of great work, pleasing to anyone's eye sounded so farfetched. At the same time, Johnny and Jake were still laughing together as if to say that there was pleasure in that place. The question of purpose was etched on both men's minds.

If their lives were part of a work in progress, then when would the finished product be viewed? What does it all mean? One thing was certain for both men. Their meeting was not an accident.

THE BARS OPEN

Four months went by much faster than Jake ever thought. He was escorted to the warden's office around nine o'clock that Monday morning. It was a bright sunny day with hardly a cloud in sight. The idea of wearing civilian clothes seemed like a real treat, but leaving without saying goodbye to Johnny saddened his heart. Thoughts of freedom permeated his mind, but the joy would have been even more real if Johnny was leaving as well. As long as his friend occupied that cell, a part of Jake would be there as well.

Jake entered the warden's office with his hands and feet free of any shackles. Ankle versions allowed him to perform his work duties without the ability to escape. They were removed when in the cell. He felt a measure of freedom before the final doors to the prison were opened. The familiar "click-thunk" sound of his cell door closing would be etched in his mind for some time. Those bars were a constant reminder of his stay and yet, somehow, they would not represent a cage of isolation. Jake thought about that first day, when Johnny took the place of another inmate. He recalled the words of the judge, the Bible, and the many discussions that followed. Now he was about to be free. The moment was bittersweet.

"So Jake, you are about to be released," the warden exclaimed.
"Yeah!"
"I really like you, Jake. You were a model prisoner."
"Thanks, warden, sir."
"Have you thought about what you would like to do with your life, Jake?"
"I have enjoyed working on the roofs, but I think something in the plumbing field would be good."

"Either area suits you, Jake. I had a lot of good reports from my guards about your work here."
"I tried to do my best, sir. I did not want a different work detail."
"You did that, Jake. You did that for sure. On the table over there are some clothes for you to wear."

Jake walked over to the table, picked up the clothes and was escorted to a changing room. There was something about stripes that no longer had any appeal. The navy blue T-shirt and denim blue jeans felt dressy in comparison to the prison wear, which he left laying on the bench in the changing room. Even the smell of the clothes matched the spring air fragrance. Jake had shaved that morning and looked like a completely new man upon leaving that room.

"How's that feel Jake," the warden asked.
"I'm ready for the nightlife, sir. These duds seem way to fancy."
"Jake, you are ready for the real world. Your stay here was but a brief detour. Any comment?"
"What's going to happen to Johnny, sir?
"We're reviewing his case now. He only has two months left. I also know that you two have become quite good friends here."
"Johnny is like a brother I never had, sir."
"Judge Carter was right about you two. He saw something in both of you, and asked if I would have you celled together."
"I know, sir. Judge Carter told me in his visit."
"So, Jake. How did that visit go? He showed me the Bible that he was going to give you."
"There was not a lot to do in a jail cell, sir, so the Bible became a source of conversation."
"Jake, I want you to know that my guards spoke often about your after lights out conversations with very good remarks. Those times were a welcomed relief from the usual name calling and vulgar language usage. When I see Judge Carter again, I need to tell him that."
"He really cares about Johnny and me, doesn't he, Warden?"
"I think Judge Carter will never retire, just because he enjoys his work. He hopes that he makes a difference in every life that

comes before him, and the words in that Bible are evident in the way he lives."

"I can see that, sir"

"Now Jake, there are a few things that we need to go over before you leave us."

"Jake, I noticed that you have added a tattoo since your arrival. A lot of felons do something like that, but why a ball and chain?"

"It is a symbol of being shackled, warden. I have been held back all my life."

"That does not have to be the case forever, Jake. You can start right now and take control of your life."

"I hope you are right, sir. I would like to make a difference someday like Judge Carter."

"You picked a fine role model, Jake."

"He is the father that I never had, sir. I would like to look him up when I get out."

"Before you leave, you need to know about your probationary period, Jake."

"I wondered about that, sir."

"Parole Officer George Patterson will be assigned to your case. You will report to h m on a regular basis over the next two years. You may feel a sense of freedom when you leave this institution, Jake, but any violation could make you a guest again. Do you understand, son?

"Yes, sir."

Jake had a brief moment of de-ja-vu, when the warden referred to Jake as "Son." Somehow, it had a measure of respect attached and Jake felt it. The idea of being anyone's son was still foreign to Jake.

The ball and chain tattooed on his right ankle became a symbol of pride. He couldn't wait to put on shorts and display it. Somehow, the tattoo had a sense of prestige or power assigned to it. The incarceration would be a weight that would always go with him. He was not proud of it, but he also wanted it etched in his memory. Prison was hard, but not unbearable. The life of gangs and drugs had a four-month hiatus.

The barb-wired gates began to slide open, first the inner one, and then the outer gate. Two guards and the warden escorted Jake. Waiting outside was his mom and stepdad. His mother had a smile from ear to ear that touched his heart. His stepfather did not appear as exuberant, but began to walk towards him.

> *"So how'd they treat you in there, Jake? You look like you've lost a couple pounds,"* his stepfather remarked.
> *"The food's not as good as mom's cooking, but they treated me well."*
> *It's so good to see you, son,"* his mother said with a huge beaming smile.
> *"Its so good to see you too, mom. I thought you would come and visit me."*
> *"We thought about it a lot, but then we thought a visit might make you even more homesick."*
> *"Judge Carter came. He was my only visitor. He gave me this Bible, mom."*

Jake held the Bible up with such pride, that his mother felt some relief. She had some feelings of regret for not making the trip, while Jake was there.

> *"That was nice of the judge, Jake."*
> *"I'll say. No one ever treated me like that. He actually cares about me. He even had Johnny assigned to my cell."*
> *"Okay, who's Johnny?"*
> *"Mom, Johnny is a new friend, a great friend. He has two months left in his sentence. When he gets out I hope we can get together. We have been studying the Bible together."*
> *"Johnny sounds like a good friend by the way you are talking about him."*
> *"He is mom. You'd like him. I think our paths were meant to cross. Its sad that it took prison to do that."*
> *"Well, Jake, get in the car and we can talk about everything on the ride home,"* his stepfather said.

Jake threw a small bag of items in the trunk, given to him during his separation process, and sat in the back seat of the family sedan. The car pulled away from the prison, while Jake peered through the rear window. His thoughts seemed to focus on Johnny, yet he wanted to capture the image of the institution from the outside. It was the first time he saw the complex during daylight hours as it was near dark when the busload of prisoners arrived. For four months, the gray walls inside had etched a different picture.

It was now Friday and spending the weekend with his mom was all Jake could think about. He had served his time, but what lay ahead? He would take things one day at a time, ever hopeful that he could someday be the kind of man that he saw in Judge Carter. There was something about that visit in the prison that produced a high, unlike anything else in Jake's life.

> *"So mom. Is Dawg going to meet us?"*
> *"Aaron has a small apartment near the warehouse, where he is working."*
> *"Wow! Dawg has a job?"*
> *"I think he stocks shelves, but he plans on becoming a manager there."*
> *"I can picture him as a stock boy, but manager? Now there's a strange thought."*
> *"He makes enough to support his apartment and drives a small pickup truck."*
> *"Did he say when he was coming over? I missed him."*
> *"He'll be over before you know it. He said that he wanted to see you as well."*

The trip home was filled with relief and expectation. The life Jake knew for four months was about to change. Any bed would be more comfortable than the prison cot. The conversation continued throughout the ride. There was so much to talk about. It seemed as though they arrived at Jake's new home seconds after they left the prison.

THE ADJUSTMENT

The family sedan pulled into the driveway of a small modular home. The outside was well maintained with a barrage of brightly colored flowers lining the front. It was a stark contrast from the gray walls of prison. Jake's room was on one end, with the kitchen and dining areas separating him from his parents. He had his own bathroom, stocked with towels and other linens. His parents moved there less than a week before he was released and felt it would offer him a fresh start as well.

The housing division was less than a mile from a shopping mall and about every other business. A twenty-six inch three-speed bicycle from the attached shed could easily get Jake where he wanted to go, as he did not have a vehicle of his own. A car was a luxury that Jake would have to earn, and he would have to find a way to do just that.

> *"What do you think of your room, Jake?"*
> *"I like the fact that I have some privacy, mom."*
> *"We selected this model, because of that feature. I'm glad you approve."*
> *"So where are we, mom?"*
> *"We are about twenty miles east of the city, but there are plenty of things to do here. They give folks our age a break on the expenses as well."*
> *"I need to find a job, mom. My parole officer will ask me what I have been doing every week, and I need to give him something constructive."*
> *"You will, Jake. You will. How 'bout some chicken and dumplings first?"*

Jake's mom was so happy to have her son home that any talk about leaving needed to be tabled. Her son was now free, and the pot on the stove held an aroma that even Jake could not refuse. It was the first time the family sat down and ate a meal together for over four months.

> "So Jake," his stepfather began. "I heard that you enjoy working with your hands. I met a man in a local coffee shop who could use a helper."
> "What does he do?"
> "He has a plumbing business and I think he does quite well. Are you interested in talking to him?"
> "I would like that, Dad."

There was a sudden lull in the conversation. Jake had never referred to his stepfather as "Dad" before. That one word may have been a Freudian slip but brought enormous satisfaction to his parents. Jake's dad took a moment to gather his thoughts. He wondered if Jake had changed during his prison stay. Did he learn respect, like a recruit in the army? Was it because his stepfather tried to provide a helping hand to him through employment contacts? Was this a sign that things would be better in the family relationships?

> "I told Jerry that you would talk to him next week. His office is just down the street"
> "Sounds good, Jake replied. "Have you got any cold beer in the fridge? I could use one right now.
> "I think there are a few cans left. Help yourself. When you get a job, you can stock it for yourself."

The initial trip home had more highs than lows. Jake was glad to have his freedom but was also anxious to get his life back in order. Up to now eighteen years has been quite chaotic. The home cooked meal and cold beer were a welcomed relief to be sure, but the idea of not having money or a car maintained its grip on Jake. Working for Jerry as a plumber's helper at least offered hope.

Jake's stepfather made sure that Jake was up before seven that Monday morning. He promised Jerry that he would bring him down to talk to him about a job as soon as the office was open. Jake must have anticipated the wake up call, as he was showered, shaved, and dressed when the rap on the door came.

"Time to get up, Jake."
"I'm up and ready, Sarge." Once again Jake offered a sign of respect. A wry smile could be seen on his stepfather's face.
"Jerry opens a bit before eight, so we can leave as soon as you have some breakfast."

The smell of bacon and eggs was another welcomed relief for Jake. He had often complained about the prison food, especially the eggs. The cooks there knew only one way to cook them, with shells and without taste. One bite of mom's eggs and Jake was instantly reunited to just how good eggs were. Creamed beef on toast was his breakfast of choice in prison, which at least offered some carbs to burn off during the work details.

The two men headed down to the plumbing office. As they arrived, Jerry was unlocking the front door.

"Hey, Jerry."
"Did ya bring Jake?"
"That's why we are here. Got any work for the boy?"
"I got a lot of work, more than I can handle. Come on in." "Go ahead Jake, I'll park the car."

The outside of the shop was not the most eloquent, but after all, plumbing work was not considered to be a very clean profession. Inside the shop were scattered boxes and plumbing fixtures that obscured the display of faucets hung off of pegboard. The boxes appeared to be from a package delivery, indicating that there was a lot of work to be done.

"So Jake, have you done any plumbing work?
"I've replaced toilets and sinks, run drain lines, soldered copper pipes, and a lot more. I enjoy it, too, Jake replied."
"That's good, because I can use someone to do all of those things. Can you start today?"
"Sure can," Jake acknowledged.
"Jake, I want you to know that I am aware of your prison record. I have had my run-ins with the law a time or two myself. If you work for me, just do your best. That's all I ask."

Those were the words that Jake needed to hear. He was worried about getting a job with his record. His salary was not even mentioned, and he forgot to ask. All he could think about was doing the work asked of him and doing it well.

> *"See that stack of boxes over there, Jake? Grab that dolly and wheel them out to the loading area in the back. I will pull my truck around to load them up."*
> *"You got it, sir."*
> *"Let's get one thing straight right now, Jake. You don't call me sir. This is not the army."*
> *"Okay, boss."*

Jerry smiled. He had been so used to working alone, that the idea of being called a "boss" seemed foreign. Yet, he was fine with it. That morning the two men loaded the truck and started out to a new housing tract. The first house was ready for the toilets and vanities to be installed. The small half bath was assigned to Jake, while the master bedroom's bath became Jerry's task. After all of the fixtures were unloaded, both men began their work. Jake completed the small bathroom and went up to get new instructions. Jerry was struggling with the toilet and nothing else was done.

> *"You done already,"* Jerry acknowledged.
> *"Piece of cake, boss. Can I help you here?"*
> *"I can't get this o-ring to seat and my back is killing me, Jake. See what you can do."*

With that, Jerry stood up and handed the duties over to Jake.

> *"I'll take care of this, boss. You can check my work downstairs."*
> *"I'll do that Jake. I could use a smoke anyway."*

Jerry left and Jake began to remove the toilet to see what was the problem with the seal. One thing was painfully obvious to Jake, judging by what he found with that toilet. Jerry was not good at what he does. The wax ring was improperly installed, the leveling screws were stripped, and the tank seal was poorly made. He went down to the truck to get a new seal and some leveling screws, when he passed Jerry outside having a smoke.

> *"How's that bath look, boss?"*

*"You did a good job, Jake. Take care of the other fixtures while
I line up the next stop."*
"Where do you keep the wax rings and leveling screws, boss?"

Jerry took Jake to a side compartment on his truck, where the
miscellaneous hardware was kept. By the end of the day, Jake had completed
four houses, all with quality results. By the end of the week, he was on
his own with the company truck, while Jerry worked the office. After each
day's work, Jerry would make his rounds to inspect the work done. Final
sign-offs needed to be done by a licensed plumber. Friday night came, and
Jerry asked Jake to join him for a brew at a local bar a couple of blocks from
the office, which he accepted.

"Whose your new friend, Jerry?" the bartender inquired. It
was obvious that Jerry was a regular visitor there.
"This is Jake. He's my new hired hand."
*"I can't believe anyone would want to work for you, you old
goat,"* the bartender snickered.
*"He done good this week. I think I am getting too old for this
stuff anyway."*
*"You are right about the getting old part. What can I get for
you boys?"*
"Whataya have, Jake? I'm buying."
"A draft is fine, boss."
"Hey! Work is over. I'm not your boss right now."

Jerry said that with a sheepish grin on his face. Then he handed Jake an
envelope with three hundred and fifty dollars inside.

*"Jake, I know we didn't discuss money when I hired you, but I
hope this is okay for now. You need to sign some form to get you
officially on the payroll. I think they call it a 1099."*

Jake looked inside the envelope and saw six fifties, two twenties and a ten
inside. *"Thank you boss,"* he replied. Jake wondered if he would always be
paid in cash. The money looked so good as it was the first he had seen since
leaving the prison.

*I know what you are thinking, Jake. Once I get the books
straightened out, I will have you on the payroll. I intended to*

pay about eight dollars an hour to start, but if you keep up the good work, I'm sure I can do better."

Eight dollars was twice the minimum wage and more than Jake had hoped for to start. The idea of working hard for higher rewards was foreign as well. Selling drugs required little effort and the money came in big lumps. Jake also thought about his parole officer. He would meet with him the next morning and having employment was a huge relief.

After a couple of hours in the bar, Jake wanted to leave, but Jerry insisted that he stay. From the conversation with the bartender, it was obvious to Jake that Jerry was a regular customer. It was also obvious that if he stayed, the words "last call" would be heard around two the next morning. Visiting his parole officer the next morning with a hangover was not a welcomed thought.

"You stay if you want, but I have other things to do tonight. See you on Monday."
"Just one more beer, Jake."
"I've had enough. I can walk home, as it is only about six blocks. If I drink anymore, it may feel like six miles."
"Suit yourself, Jake. See ya Monday."

The first week out of the pen was far better than Jake had anticipated. Still, he could not stop thinking about Johnny. When he arrived home that Friday night, his parents asked how his day went, and seemed pleasantly surprised by his reaction.

THE REPORT

This has been a good week, Jake thought to himself as he laid his head on the pillow. He had thought a lot about what his life on the outside would be like from his prison cell. Incarceration allows for times of reflection of where you have been as well as the path you might take down the road. A life of crime, drugs, and alcohol had filled his past, but the events of his first week of freedom offered a different direction. Working for a man like Jerry did not enter his thoughts in prison. In fact, holding any job above minimum wage sounded pretty far-fetched.

Each night, when he laid down, there seemed to be a peace that he never felt before. It was not uncommon to wake up in his cell with the sheet and blanket wadded up at one end. But, at home, Jake woke in the same position as he started. The restless nights had disappeared, at least for a time. That was true on that first Saturday morning after leaving the prison. Jake had a nine o'clock appointment with his parole officer, and was up by seven. The smell of bacon cooking was another incentive. The bike ride would only take about ten minutes, but Jake left the house before eight-thirty.

Jake parked his bike near a chain-linked fence, located in the rear of a three-story building. George Patterson's office was listed as room 312. After securing his bike to the fence with a chain and padlock, Jake entered the building. Behind the glass entrance was a listing of businesses and the floors they were on. *Patterson Correctional Services"* was listed under the third floor column, so Jake took the stairs up two flights. It was not difficult finding George's office, as it was directly across from the stairway when he reached the top. Jake was about twenty minutes early, but the door to the office was unlocked. He stepped inside and sat down in the waiting area.

There were six cushioned chairs and three end tables in the room. Another door with George's name was off to the side. Jake could see that the lights were on, but he waited until the clock on the wall neared nine before knocking. Various magazines were scattered on the tables, and he began to scan through them. He was not much into sports and gardening, but a bodybuilding magazine caught his eye. Jake was six feet tall and about two hundred pounds, but his six-pack had become a bit flabby. Still, if you met him in an alley, you would want him on your side.

Around the room were other interesting items, which he noticed. There were two cameras mounted at the ceiling in opposite corners of the waiting area. He wondered what they were there for as no one would want to rob the place. A corkboard with several photographs was hung near the front door. Curious, he went over to examine the pictures to see if his mug was on display. The board was pretty full, but he could not locate his picture. As he was staring, a voice called him.

> *"Hey, Jake."* George had opened his door and spotted him.
> *"Hi, Mr. Patterson."*
> *"Do you remember me?"*
> *"I thought it might be you, except I was about thirteen. You asked me a lot of questions about my childhood."*
> *"Dick Buttons was your assigned officer back then, but we shared a lot of cases together."*
> *"I thought Dick had a cushy job and his belly reflected it."*
> *"He did like to eat. I'll give you that, Jake. I see that you are here early for your appointment. I will be with you in a moment."*

Jake acknowledged with a nod and sat down to continue scanning his magazine. George was about the same height as Jake, but thirty or forty pounds lighter. He wasn't wearing any form of uniform, so if Jake had met him on the street, he would not have associated him with a law enforcement officer. His voice was soft but distinctive. Somehow, Jake had pictured a much bigger man with a rough voice, stereotypical of someone in authority. He didn't put two and two together until after he saw George and recognized him from a meeting five years earlier.

A few minutes later the door opened and another man was leaving in front of Mr. Patterson. Jake recognized him immediately.

"Hi Warden Carter."
"Hi Jake. How's life treating you?"
"Fine, Warden. I have a job."
"Really! That's wonderful, Jake."
"Yeah! I'm a plumber's assistant."
"That is the perfect job for you Jake. Well, I have to leave, but you are in good hands with Mr. Patterson here."

Warden Carter walked over to Jake and reached out his hand. Jake stood and gave him a solid shake. There is something about the way a man grips in a handshake that speaks volumes. The warden's grip was strong, but somehow gentle at the same time. Jake felt a real sense of caring in the exchange. Whatever the two men shared behind closed doors could not have been too bad. Then the warden smiled, which solicited a grin from Jake as well.

"See you in two weeks, Warden," George acknowledged.
"Don't forget our golf game on Tuesday, George."
"I won't. I am looking forward to taking your money, Warden."
"Someday I will beat you. Good luck on your meeting Jake. This is your first one since being free, isn't it?
"Yes, warden. Thanks."
"Come on in, Jake. We've got a lot to talk about."

With those words, Jake entered the office. It was nearly wall-to-wall filing cabinets, with stacks of folders piled on the desk. If neatness was a virtue, then George is a long way from perfection. Yet, with all the clutter, somehow, this parole officer knew where things were. If he had a system, it was not obvious. Lying alone on the center of the desk was a folder with Jake's name on it, along with his prison snapshot. George sat down behind his desk and motioned for Jake to sit facing him.

"So Jake, what's going on with your life?"
"I'm working, Mr. Patterson."
"That's great, but you can call be George. My friends also call me Harley."
"Harley? Where did you get that name?"
"I used to have a motorbike and rode with a bunch of leatherjackets."

> *"You were a Hell's Angel? I just can't picture that."*
> *"We were a rather motley gang, but nothing destructive. We just liked to ride together."*
> *"Do you still ride, Harley?"*
> *"Every chance I get. Now tell me about your week."*
> *"I started working for a plumber. I really enjoy it."*
> *"That's great. How did you get that job?*
> *"My dad set it up."*
> *"So tell me, Jake, how did that happen?"*
> *"I'm not sure, Harley. I think he knew that I could do that kind of work. Maybe, my mom told him."*
> *"Interesting! Warden Carter told me that you did not have a good relationship with your father, or should I say stepfather?"*
> *"We were not close, if that's what you mean, but he's different now."*
> *"He's different, Jake? Do you think that you might be different?"*

Jake took a moment to reflect on that concept. Surely, four months of prison can change a person, but is that what happened here, he pondered. Had he learned something about respect under Warden Carter? Perhaps, his stepfather was the one, who made the change. After some thought, he responded:

> *"I think I see things differently now. I think I changed the most, but my family did as well."*
> *"Jake, I want you to know that your parents were kept informed all during your incarceration. Warden Carter keeps in contact with family members. I'm sure that he told them about your work at the prison, and that is how your father sought work for you to do when you got out."*

Jake's parents never came to see him during his stay, but the fact that they were being informed helped Jake begin to understand why. He served his time and was a model prisoner. Those facts must have been a great comfort to his parents, who may not have wanted to jeopardize his progress by a visit. Perhaps, if his sentence were considerably longer, they would have come. Still, learning that his parents were kept abreast of things came as a small shock. Without that correspondence, he may not have gotten the work he was now doing, so he was grateful.

> *"How do you like your new home, Jake? The warden told me that your parents had moved."*
> *"I like it, Harley. I have my own bath and I am close to the kitchen. What more do I need?"*
> *"After showering with the inmates, your own bath must seem pretty good, huh?"* George found it difficult to hide his wry smile.
> *"You bet. Mom's home cooking is pretty good, too."*
> *"Jake, the warden's report on you is something out of a fairy tale. He could only hope that all his inmates behaved like you. I was impressed as I read it."*
> *"I think I thought things in the joint would be quite different, Harley, but I liked my work and my cellmate."*
> *"I guess if you have good friends and like what you do, then not much else matters."*
> *"You could say that. I am looking forward to doing more plumbing jobs next week. I think I am pretty good at it."*
> *"According to Warden Carter, you are very good. I think he might hire you to take care of some things around his house as well."*
> *"Tell him, anytime."*
> *"I'll do that next week on the golf course, Jake. By the way, did you hear from Johnny?"*

Jake went from a moment of lighthearted laughter to one of remorse. The mention on Johnny's name brought sadness. He could not stop thinking about his friend's time in prison. Did they put someone else in his cell? If so, did they get along? Did anyone bring Johnny a Bible? At that moment he looked up and said:

> *"Hey, Harley. Could you do something for me? "What's that, Jake?"*
> *"Could you get a Bible to Johnny. We enjoyed reading it together and I am sure he would like one."*
> *"I could, but why don't you give it to him yourself?"*

"I don't have a car, and the bike ride would take hours."
"Johnny is going to be released on Monday, Jake."
"How can that be? Doesn't he have about eight more weeks to his sentence?"
"The warden has commuted his sentence and assigned me as his parole officer."
"But, how did that happen?"
"You did it, Jake. You did it."
"How could I do anything to help Johnny?"
"The letters from the warden to your parents also talked a lot about Johnny and your relationship. Your parents persuaded the warden that continuing that relationship could best heal Johnny's anger. I hope you will like your new roommate, Jake."

Those words were like a breath of fresh air. The feelings he had for his parents were now more loving than ever. They cared enough about him to also help his new best friend. Monday was only two days away. Jake could not wait to see Johnny again. He was like a boy anticipating a day at Disney World.

"Jake, do me a favor and pin your mug shot on the board before you leave. Will you do that?
"Sure thing, Harley."

Each time Jake spoke the name, Harley, a chuckle came with it. The picture of George riding with "The Hell's Angels" seemed comical to say the least. There was no long beard, obvious tattoos, or beer belly. George was not the stereotypical biker. Sometimes, things are not what they seem to be. Jake had treated his stepfather as a drill sergeant with strict rules of conduct in the past. After hearing what he did to help locate employment and bring Johnny home, he was forming a new impression that included a caring spirit. He had given up on men, especially those in fatherly roles. Now, he was beginning to feel a love that he never truly felt before. It felt good.

He pinned his photo on the board, and turned back towards Harley.

"Same time next week, Harley."
"Same time, Jake, at least for a while."

He unlocked his bike, jumped on, and began pedaling as fast as he could back home. He couldn't wait to confront his parents about Johnny. His first meeting with his parole officer went far better than he ever imagined. Although there was some discussion behind closed doors about behavior, goals, and expectations, the focus was on how well Jake has adapted back into society. Whatever he was doing was okay as far as Harley was concerned. Judge Carter's warm handshake offered additional confirmation.

Jake arrived home, while his mother was outside working in her flower garden.

> *"Mom. Mom. They told me that Johnny was coming here on Monday."*
>
> *"That was going to be a surprise, Jake. Your dad and I are picking him up at noon on Monday."*
>
> *"I sure wish I could be there with you guys."*
>
> *"Johnny will be here when you get off work, Jake. You need to work."*
>
> *"I couldn't believe it when Harley told me the news."*
>
> *"Harley, Who's Harley?"*
>
> *"Oh, that's George my parole officer. He likes to ride Harley Davidson bikes. I can't believe Johnny's getting out."*
>
> *"Your father has had a lot of conversations with Warden Carter about Johnny's release."*
>
> *"Where is Dad, mom?"*
>
> *"He went to get a few groceries, Jake. He will be back shortly."*

Jake sat down on the front step and awaited his father's return.

RENEWAL

In some ways, Jake was like a mature thirty-year-old man. At other times he was still a small child. Waiting on those steps showed signs of both. The excitement building inside him about Johnny's release was like a child in a candy store. As he waited, he couldn't stop thinking about what his stepfather had done on Johnny's behalf. For the first time, he felt like a son. He began to think about all of the manipulation that he had used against his stepfather and felt genuine sorrow.

The car pulled in the driveway, and sarge got out carrying an armful of groceries.

> *"Can I help you, Dad?"* Jake said wit some passion.
> *"Sure, Jake. There are more bags in the trunk."*
> *"How'd your meeting wit your parole officer go?"*
> *"Great!"*

Both men carried on a dialogue as they completed their grocery tasks. Usually, only a few words were spoken in a conversation with an abrupt ending. This time it was different. Jake seemed to have a real desire to keep the communication going, and Joe enjoyed the exchange.

> *"I found out about Johnny today, Dad."*
> *"I guess the surprise element is gone now, huh, Jake?"*
> *"I was more than surprised. I think about Johnny every night. I miss our talks."*
> *"You'll have time to renew them."*
> *"'Dad'. I really would like to call you that from now on. Is that okay with you?"*

Joe began to well up inside. He loved Jake as his own son and only dreamed that some measure of respect would someday be returned. He had tried to reach him on many levels in the past, but now he asked himself the question, "Why now?" Was Jake's spirit of rebellion broken, like one of Joe's enlisted men? Did prison have that great an influence? Joe had more questions than answers.

> *"I would love for you to call me 'Dad', son."*
> *"Dad, I am so sorry for the way I have treated you all these years. Please forgive me."*
> *"You bet. So, Jake, what brought all of this on?"* Joe wanted to probe deeper to get some closure on his own internal dialog.
> *"I think I just grew up, Dad. Harley shared a lot of things with me today."*
> *"Harley?"*
> *"Yeah! He's my parole officer. That's his nickname."*
> *"I guess there is another story about that, huh?"*
> *"Mom can share it with you. Anyway, I learned about the letters you and mom received from Judge Carter during my prison stay."*
> *"He sure is a great man."*
> *"He cares about people, doesn't he, Dad?"*
> *"I think so. I know that he cares about you. We were so impressed by how you handled yourself in there. We wanted to visit you, but thought it might, somehow, change things. Judge Carter told us to wait."*
> *"I wondered why he was the only visitor I had. I thought Dawg, or you guys would make the trip."*
> *"We shared together with Aaron and he also agreed to stay away."*
> *"It was through those letters that you helped find work for me, wasn't it, dad?"*
> *"Judge Carter said you had great potential as a carpenter of plumber. I just asked around."*
> *"After all the trouble I have caused you, Dad, you did that for me?"*

"Yes. You may not believe it, but I have always loved you. When I married your mother, I let her know that we would somehow be a family. I cherish this day as I feel that dream has come true."

"For an army sergeant you are becoming soft, Dad." Jake said this, because there was a stream of tears flowing down Joe's face. It was another defining moment for them both.

"Don't tell anyone. My reputation is at hand you know." Joe snickered.

"When Harley told me that Johnny was coming to live with us, my heart wanted to beat out of my chest. I couldn't believe what I was hearing."

"Did you know that your mom and I went to visit Johnny?"

"No. When did you do that?"

"We received a letter from the warden two days after your release and called to set up a meeting the next day. After the meeting, the warden said that it would be good to have a conversation with Johnny."

"So how was Johnny?"

"I think he was okay, but he sure talked a lot about you. He missed your late night discussions."

"Yeah! I miss them, too."

"The warden did not place anyone new in his cell. Judge Carter felt that serving the remainder of his time with us would be more productive. He thought well of Johnny as you know."

"So, will Johnny have to look for a job?"

"He will be helping us around the house. I think he has to wear some contraption for the remainder of his sentence as part of the release criteria, but that shouldn't be more than a few weeks. What he will do afterwards is pretty much up to him. He may want to go home."

"This can be his home."

"He has family somewhere, Jake. We just agreed to completing his sentence with us."

Jake was still in shock about what happened this day. Seeing Johnny again was all he could think about. They would have a lot to talk about. Monday evening could not come quickly enough.

> *"Hey dad. I would like to do something before Johnny arrives."*
> *"What is that, Jake?"*
> *"Could you take me someplace where I can purchase a Bible?"*
> *"How about after lunch, Jake. I think mom has a great meal planned."*
> *"That'll work, dad."*

The two men went inside the house, as lunch was about ready. The conversation around that table was so uplifting that Joe picked up numerous winks from his wife. Each one came with a confirmation that they had made a good decision about Johnny. It was a decision that deeply touched Jake's heart. Their actions spoke far more than any words.

Before lunch was over, Aaron arrived unannounced.

> *"Smells good, mom."*
> *"Have a seat. There's plenty left, Aaron."*
> *"What's happening? Everyone seems to be in such a great mood."*

The normal snide remarks and subtle innuendos were obviously missing. Aaron sensed the difference almost immediately.

> *"Dawg, Johnny's going to stay with us starting on Monday."*
> *"You mean your prison pal?"*
> *"Mom and dad worked out a deal to get him released in their home."*
> *"That's nice, Jake. I know how much you like Johnny."*
> *"I guess mom and dad knew that too, huh?"*
> *"Yeah! They're great people. They took me in, didn't they?"*

With that, no more words needed to be uttered. After the meal, Jake and Joe drove down to a Christian store to look at Bibles.

> *"Do you know what Bible to buy, Jake? There are many versions."*
> *"I think I will get one just like mine called, 'The Living Bible.'*

Then I want to mark the same verses that are highlighted in mine."
"That shouldn't be hard to find. It was a pretty popular version, because it was closer to our English."

Within an hour, they returned with the Bible. Jake used a small portion of his first wages to make the purchase and felt good about it. He worked hard for something, and for the first time, felt true satisfaction. His life of crime would gain money to buy things, but prior to this, there was no real sense of ownership. Drugs, alcohol, or other commodities would come and go, but this Bible marked something with lasting value. It was a new experience to be sure.

The rest of the weekend seemed to drag. When Monday morning came, Jake was up at the crack of dawn. He had to stop at the plumbing office to pick up some fixtures for the day's assignments, but the office was still closed for at least an hour. He had placed his Bible in the front seat of the company van and picked it up to read, while waiting for Jerry to show. Jerry had not trusted him yet with a key. While he read, he could not shake the thought about being created for a purpose, namely to do God's work. The events of that past weekend seemed surreal. He kept waiting for someone to wake him up. At the end of the day, he would be reunited with his friend.

Jerry arrived a few minutes early and unlocked the office.

"Pull the van around back, Jake and load up. I have a lot of worked planned for you.
"Yes, sir, I mean boss." Jake had hoped that the work would be a little lighter, so he could go home earlier.
"Here's the deal, Jake. I decided to pay you by the job. The more you do, the more you make. You should do a lot better than the eight dollars an hour rate. What do you think?"
"So, what have you got planned to do today?"
"Here is a list of homes to do complete this week, Jake. Two of them per day should work."

Jake looked at the list of tasks. Tubs and showers take the longest. Vanities and toilets are a piece of cake. The first two homes had mostly faucets. The showers and tubs were completed, except for these fixtures, so he knew that he could easily complete those homes quickly. Beside each line item was a dollar amount.

> *"Is this what you are paying me for each service, boss?"*
> *"That's correct, Jake. Do you think it's fair?*
> *"More than fair."*
> *"Good. That helps me quote jobs in the future. If it takes you longer, you will earn less per hour. But, if you are done sooner, you earn more. That works for me as well."*
> *"Me too, boss."*

If Jake completed the first two houses that day, he would earn over eighty dollars. If he were done early, then he would see Johnny sooner. He couldn't wait to get started. The work went very smoothly and both homes were done before three that afternoon. Earning money this way seemed much better than the life of crime that he knew. He also had a sense of accomplishment. He took great pride in completing each task. Shortly after three he arrived home, expecting to see Johnny, but his parents were not there yet.

He contemplated a barrage of questions. What if something happened and Johnny was not released? Maybe, some inmates who learned about it beat him? Then he remembered how much paperwork and final preparations were necessary during his release, and felt more at ease. Usually, when he had internalized questions, they were all tilted to the negative side. But, this time there was some balance. It was almost eerie. He did not feel the nervous anxiety that he had felt in the past. It was as if he was enclosed in a protective dwelling place, with the worldly concerns unable to penetrate.

Shortly after four PM, his parents pulled into the driveway. Johnny had his window down and was yelling as soon as he saw his friend.

> *"Jake. Jake. It's really you."*

Jake could not wait for the car to stop moving. He ran to grab Johnny's hand through the window.

> *"You're here, Johnny. I can't believe you're actually here."*
> *"You got some great parents, Jake."*

"You don't have to tell me that. I know." The words caused instant smiles on Joe and his mom.

"Johnny. It's so great to see you again. I really missed you."

"I missed you too, Jake. I just can't believe I am here with you now."

"Grab your bag Johnny and take it to Jake's room. Jake will help you get settled," his mom shouted.

"I have an airbed on the floor for you, Johnny. Its not the Ritz, but I am sure it beats the prison bed. Besides, you had the bottom bunk, so you should feel right at home. Both men grinned simultaneously.

"I think anything would be better than that bunk, Jake."

"I got something for you, Johnny." Jake reached under his pillow and pulled out the new Bible that he purchased and handed it to Johnny. *"This is for you. I even marked the same verses that were marked in my book."*

Tears streamed down Johnny's cheeks. It was a gift that touched Johnny for a lifetime. Johnny had held so much anger after his father left, leaving his mother crying for weeks. But, his tears were tears of joy. The book was a treasure as it reminded him of the many hours of sharing the two men had in the prison cell. The very judge that highlighted special verses also played a role in uniting the two men. The reunion was almost complete. All that was left was the time they would spend sharing together, only this time there would be no call for lights out.

CONVERSATIONS

There was something mystical about the reunion between Jake and Johnny. The words highlighted in chapter two of Ephesians seemed to take on new meaning to both men.

For we are God's masterpiece. He has created us anew in Christ Jesus, so we can do the good things he planned for us long ago.

Johnny did not want to talk about anything related to prison. He had memorized the words in Ephesians and thought long about what they meant. Things had happened in his life, both good and bad, but there was always the nagging "Why?" questions. If the anger that raged inside of him was for a reason, then he needed to know why. Why was he placed in Jake's cell? Why did Jake's parents agree to the house arrest terms? That question had significant merit, because nothing had been done like that before, at least not to Johnny's knowledge. There was something about that verse that screamed for an answer.

"Jake. Are you asleep?"
"Its midnight Johnny. I thought we were all talked out an hour ago."
"I know. I can't stop thinking about that verse."
"What verse?"
"Ephesians 2:10. Have you thought much about your life since you got out?"
"All the time, Johnny. Prison sure changes things, or maybe things sure have changed on the outside. Mom and dad changed a lot."

"Maybe you are the one that has done most of the changing, Jake. Have you thought of that?"

"Yeah! I know I have changed. I have no desire for the drug scene."

"It says that we are God's 'masterpiece.' The things we have gone through in our past were not accidents. They were intentional brush strokes in our lives. Then He says that our past experiences will be used for good."

"You're here with me now, aren't you, Johnny. I think that's pretty good. Now go to sleep."

"That's very good, but don't you see? All this was planned in advance for our benefit."

"If that's true, Johnny, did He plan for us to not get any sleep tonight?"

"I'm sorry, Jake. Thanks for listening. Good night."

The conversation ended, but the thoughts would stay with both men throughout Johnny's stay. It was as if a seed had been planted, a seed of wonderment that needed nurturing through thoughtful discovery. Every time an event happened in either man's life, which could be classified as unusual, the event was shared. The scripture verses from Judge Carter began to grow. The process of discernment had begun.

The next morning Jake woke before the alarm went off. He jumped out of bed as usual to deactivate the alarm and completely forgot that he had a houseguest. The lump between Jake's right foot and the floor was Johnny's left leg that had fallen off the air mattress. Needless to say, Johnny also awoke.

"What the..." Johnny blurted.

"Sorry, good buddy. I guess things have changed around here."

"Good morning to you too, Jake. What time is it?"

"A few minutes after six, Johnny."

"I feel like I just got to sleep, but that's still later than the prison call."

"Go back to sleep Johnny, unless you want to try mom's cooking?"

"Is that bacon, I smell?"

"Compared to the cell, Johnny, this is the Ritz."

Johnny lay back down for a few moments, while Jake showered. The thoughts of a good home cooked meal now prevented him from regaining the deep sleep he was enjoying before the interruption. He reasoned that he could always go back to bed after Jake left for work, so why fight it? The smell of freshly cooked bacon led him into the kitchen.

"Good morning, Mama."
"Good morning, Johnny."
"I just realized that I don't know your name. Is it okay if I call you 'Mama'?"
"I'm flattered Johnny, but you can call me ' Grace'."
"Grace? That's an amazing name. Do you know that you're amazing, Grace?"
"We are all special, Johnny. Even you, but thanks for the compliment."
"That food sure smells good, Grace."

Each time Johnny uttered her name, thoughts of the conversation last night with Jake resurfaced. Johnny understood something about grace from the highlighted scripture. It had something to do with receiving something that you didn't earn. Early release to Jake's family was like an act of grace. If God had arranged that to happen, then it was His grace that was applied to Johnny's life. Still, Johnny thought the name "Grace" was no accident. If God had His hand on the lives of two prisoners, then, surely, He could also touch this family.

Johnny was like a sponge during his stay with Jake's family. He had an unquenchable thirst for answers to his "Why?" Questions. The words from Ephesians had found fertile soil in Johnny's heart. During his quest for truth, something else was also beginning. The wellspring of anger that had control of him began to dry up. The more he searched for truth, the less volatile he was in confrontations.

"How do you like your eggs, Johnny?"
"Cooked." Johnny answered with a sheepish grin.
"Jake likes his scrambled with cheese added. You want to try them that way?"

"I haven't had them made that way since I was a boy, Grace."
"Are you from the south, Johnny? I learned to cook them that way here in Florida. I think it's a southern dish."
"I grew up in Alabama. My mom moved here several years ago."
"Would you like to see your mom, Johnny?"
"That would be wonderful, Grace. She doesn't live that far away, but I don't know how to reach her."
"Warden Carter gave me her address and a work phone number. I could try and get a hold of her if you like. I was going to let her know that you were with us at any rate."
"Please do. I would love to see her. Maybe she can help me with some answers to the questions I have."

Just then, Jake entered the room.

"You eating my food, Johnny?" (Jake said with a smile.)
"You bet, Jake. Grace is a great cook." "Grace?"
"You're mom, Jake."
"Mom, I haven't heard anyone call you that in ages." "Would you prefer that Johnny call me mama?" "Grace is fine. Got any more of those vittles, Grace?" "Mom will do just fine for you Jake. Eat up."

Jake enjoyed eating breakfast with his friend. Their conversation was filled with humor and insightful comments. The warm smile on his mom's face spoke volumes. She had to interrupt the two men to keep Jake from being late for work.

"We'll talk later, Jake. Have a good day."
"You, too, Johnny. I should be back in time for supper."
"You better if you want any," Johnny said with a smirk.

Grace left a message for Johnny's mother at her workplace that morning. The returned call came around noon. Address information was exchanged along with a time to meet. Johnny's mom would be coming over sometime after four that afternoon. There was real excitement in her voice. When Johnny heard the news, he jumped in the shower, shaved, and put on the best looking clothes that he had. He was looking forward to the meeting as well.

Johnny buried himself that afternoon in the lounge chair in the living room, along with his new Bible. Then the doorbell rang. It was a quarter to four. Mom was early, which helped limit the anxiety inside Johnny. Grace answered the door, exchanged greetings, and invited her inside. Johnny had already stood and started walking towards his mother. She was a small lady, wearing a dress that may have lost its style ten or fifteen years ago.

> *"Mom! You look terrific."* Johnny said as he ran to give her a hug.
> *"Johnny. Johnny."* She threw her arms out to accept the embrace.
> *"I missed you so much. What a handsome man you've become."*
> *"Mom. I am so sorry for causing you so much grief. I love you. I really love you."*

Those words penetrated deeply within her heart. How she had longed to hear them. Raising her son alone was hard enough, but any communication between them in the past had been wrought with anger. She had always felt that Johnny blamed her for the sudden loss of his father. She sensed the change in her son by his embrace and words. The tears could not stop flowing down her cheeks.

> *"Don't cry, Mama. Don't cry."*
> *"Its okay, Johnny."* Grace interjected. *Those are truly tears of joy.*
> *"I have so many things to talk about with you Mama. So many things."*
> *"I have missed so much of your life, Johnny. I would love to learn everything about you. I love you, son."*
> *"You both need to get reacquainted. I will be in the spare room getting caught up on some ironing. Can I get you something before I leave."*
> *"Some tissues might help, Grace."*

After leaving a fresh box of tissues, Grace left. Johnny and his mother began a long-awaited reunion. The questions inside began to pour out and the healing process continued. Johnny learned that his father had a drinking problem and while under the influence would beat his mother. Their divorce came after his mother feared for Johnny's life. His dad was a truck driver, but was now working on a loading dock somewhere in Oregon. Three DUI's not only lost his truck driver's license, but also landed him in jail for a month. He remarried twice, both ending in divorce.

Some of the pieces of the puzzle began to reconnect for Johnny. He wondered if the anger he had bottle up all those years was passed down from his father. Then he began to understand that it did not make a difference. He had found a way to release himself from the bondage. He also made a silent vow to avoid alcohol. The conversation turned to more recent topics.

> *"So, Mom. Where are you working?"*
> *"I am a waitress at a local family restaurant. I would love for you to stop in sometime."*
> *"I would love that, but Grace's cooking will be hard to beat."*
> *"Where do you live?"* Johnny asked.
> *"In a trailer park like this on the west side of town. Its about all I can afford."*
> *"I'm so glad that you are nearby. I always wondered why you never came to see me in prison."*
> *"I just couldn't bring myself to face you, son. I blamed myself for everything that happened to you."*
> *"You were not to blame, Mama."*
> *"When you left after high school, I thought you wanted to be with your dad."*
> *"I did want to find him. That's true, but I never blamed you."*
> *"You had so much anger, Johnny. I could only imagine that it was directed at me. You did leave. I felt responsible."*
> *"But, I kept in touch with you. I just wanted to be on my own."*
> *"I have always been grateful for that. When you moved here, I had to come as well. I just wanted to keep you near. I hated the thought of losing you. Yet, at the same time thought that I had already lost you. Does that make any sense, Johnny?"*

"Life doesn't make sense sometimes, Mama, but that is why I am here now. Through my friend Jake, I have discovered something about who I am and why I am here."

Johnny reached over to the end table and grabbed his Bible. He opened it to Ephesians and asked his mother to read verse 2:10. After she read the words, Johnny stared into her eyes with a look of such inner peace, that her heart was relieved as well.

"Don't you get it, Mama? Either we are here by accident or we have a purpose. Those words tell me that I have a purpose. So do you, Mama. So do you. We just have to find what that is."
"Johnny, I believe that you are no accident. I believe in you and desire that you find your calling in this life. Whatever that is, I am just proud to be back in your life."
"You never left, Mama. You never left."

The two were so wrapped up in getting to know each other again, that they did not notice Jake's return from work. Grace had a large crock-pot of stew prepared for the evening meal, and the aroma filled the entire house. Grace interrupted with the announcement that dinner was ready, and everyone was welcome.

"That means you, too, Mama. You get to try Grace's cooking."

The two sat down together at the dinner table. Joe was helping some friends move in a few houses down the street and would arrive later. Johnny was so moved by the day's events, that he wanted to offer a prayer before eating. Jake looked at him with some surprise as prayer was rarely heard in the household.

"Dear God. If the words in the Bible are your words, then I want to thank you for what you are doing in my life. Thank you for this family who have offered so much love to me. Thank you for allowing my mother to be here this day. Thank you for my friend, Jake, who also seems to be one of your works in progress. I don't know what the next day holds, but I look forward to seeing it unfold. Thank you for the food that is before us. This has been a great day. Thank you."
"Amen. Let's eat." Jake responded.

For the first time, Johnny had a conversation with his father, his heavenly father. If life had meaning, he was on a mission to find what it was for his life. The reunion with his mother had been a joyful one. Many of his questions had been answered. As he uttered the words in his prayer, Jake sensed the peace in his heart. The midnight conversation began to take root in Jake's heart as well, although the process would take time.

"So Jake, how was you day," Johnny asked, while Jake was chewing a mouthful of food.

"Great, Johnny. I completed three houses today, one more than my boss thought I could handle. Do you know what that means?"

"That you will be done early on Friday?"

"Maybe, but it means more money. He pays me according to the job, so I earn more when I do more jobs."

"You are good at plumbing, so that's a good way to get paid. I tried to fix a faucet once when I was about thirteen. If I got paid by the job, I think I would have made ten cents an hour that day."

"Sounds like my boss. He's a klutz. I don't know how he got his business going by the way he works. He needs me."

"It must feel pretty good to feel needed, Jake. Have you given any thought to starting your own business someday?"

"A lot. But, it will take money and a good reputation, neither of which I have at the moment."

"Keep it up and you will someday, Jake. You will."

The conversation warmed the hearts of both mothers. Grace was uplifted by the satisfaction in Jake's voice as he shared about the day's events. He truly loved his work and was good at it. Some parents may wish for their children to become doctors, engineers, or some other high paying profession. Grace just wanted her son to do something he enjoyed. Johnny's mother sensed the heartfelt friendship that existed between the two men. Good friends are hard to find. She could only hope that it would last a lifetime.

NATURE CALLS

The nightly conversations between Johnny and Jake continued over the next eight weeks. Johnny's quest for answers slowly began to penetrate Jake's mind and heart as well. Friday night conversations were usually cut short, as Jake joined his boss for a few brews after the week's work. Johnny kept true to his self-made promise to avoid alcohol and refused to join Jake, even after his house arrest had been lifted.

Jake had saved some money from his weekly pay and decided to take his friend out for some new clothes. On the last Saturday that Johnny spent at their home, he told his friend to load his few belongings into the plumbing company's van. It was time for Johnny to get more reacquainted with his mother. After both men made their weekly trip to see Harley with their parole requirements, they went to a local clothing store for some new duds. Johnny's wardrobe was limited to a couple pair of jeans and some raggedy shirts, so it was time for a fresh start. Then the two men headed off to the west side of town.

They arrived at a small family restaurant to have lunch. Johnny spotted his mother immediately and quietly positioned himself behind her. He waited until she placed the plates she was carrying down before announcing his arrival with a warm hug. Startled, she turned around and returned the favor. Jake could only look on with a warm smile of his own.

"Mama, I hear the food in this place is pretty good. What do you recommend for a couple hungry lads?"
"Hello, Jake. This meal's on me. Thanks for bringing my son."
"My pleasure, ma'am. Can you put him up for a while? He's beginning to get on my nerves with all of his chatter."

Jake tried to keep a straight face, but could not keep the sheepish grin from cracking through.

> *"Do you mean it Johnny? Do you really want to come and live with me?"*
> *"You bet, Mom. Besides, Jake snores."* Johnny returned the wry smile.
> *"Are those new clothes, Johnny?"*
> *"Jake splurged a bit on me today. I hope you like them."*

The fellowship that day was like something out of a fairy tale. Happy endings could not have been written any better. Somehow, this was not an ending, but a new beginning for everyone. Johnny would begin a new relationship with his mother, while continuing his quest for life's answers. Jake no longer was concerned about his friend. The anguish was gone from both men.

When Jake returned home, things seemed different. The air mattress was stored away, and the quietness was, somehow, deafening. Aaron stopped by and was waiting for Jake's return.

> *"Dawg. When did you get here?"*
> *"I just arrived a few minutes ago, Jake. How are you doing?"*
> *"Great."*
> *"I'm sorry that I missed seeing Johnny. How's he doing?"*
> *"Johnny's doing great. You should have seen him today with his mother. It was …well, beautiful to watch."*
> *"I thought we could do some catching up. How 'bout a brew?"*
> *"Sounds great, Dawg."*

The brothers had a lot of things to talk about. The Friday night hangout became a Saturday afternoon gab session. They talked about work, family and an occasional sporting event. But, as young adults, the conversation led to fleshly desires.

> *"Hey, Dawg. Do you have a girl?"*
> *"I have a few, but nothing serious."*
> *"Mind sharing?"* Jake snickered.
> *"Are you kidding. She'd be ruined for life if she spent even an hour with you."* Aaron returned the grin.

Just then the door opened. The sound of high heels clicking towards them captured their attention. She was about five feet six, slender, and wearing a tight leather skirt. She took a stool at the bar about ten feet from their booth. If their stares were like lasers, then she would have serious holes in her legs and leather skirt.

"Never mind, Dawg. I'll take some of that."
"You could get hurt, brother. Better let me test the merchandise out first."
"Now who's doing the ruining, Dawg?"

The conversation continued for some time until she swung around on the stool and glanced towards them. She seemed to be peering at Jake's ankle with the ball and chain tattoo. Aaron stood and motioned to the bartender for a new round of drinks. As he went to the bar to pick them up, the woman passed by and took his seat in the booth.

"Can I get you something as well?" Aaron asked.
"Whatever you are having would be fine," she responded.
 "What's your name?" Jake inquired.
"Joan. What's yours?"
"I'm Jake and that's Aaron. I call him Dawg."
"Does he bark?"
"He's my adopted brother. He lost his parents when he was a young teenager. The nickname 'Dawg' stuck one day."
"Where'd you get the tattoo?"
"I was a bad boy once."
"It looks like a prison tattoo."
"Yeah. Well I spent a few months on a weapon charge."
"Carrying now?"

As she spoke, her foot slowly moved up Jake's thigh under the booth. Before Jake could respond, Aaron returned with the drinks and sat down next to Joan.

"So, Joan. Do you come here often?"
"Occasionally, I meet my father here."
"Is he here now? Aaron asked.

"I don't see him yet, but I am sure he will be here soon enough. He lives here on weekends."
"I come in on Friday nights after work with my boss," Jake responded.
"What do you do, Jake?"
"I work in plumbing."
"That's what my dad does as well. His name is Jerry."

With that, Jake's jaw dropped. Could this voluptuous child be his boss's daughter? He never mentioned that he had a child, but then again, he never asked. Then the thought of tight leather skirts and high heels seemed to put a damper on any type of father-child relationship.

"Wow! That old codger has a daughter," Jake remarked.
"He started drinking heavy after mom died in a car accident. He was driving and fell asleep at the wheel coming home from a social event."
"When did that happen?" Jake continued.
"Seven years ago. He hasn't been the same since. He used to be the best plumber around, but that event changed him."
"Do you blame your father for your mother's death?" Aaron inserted.
"Maybe, sometimes. But I'm past all that. I come here to unwind and he's still a good listener."
"You can come here with me. I'm a good listener." Jake responded.

Joan's body language continued to arouse Jake, while Aaron felt like the odd man out. He looked at his watch and gulped down his beer as if to say it was time to leave.

"You got a fire to put out, Dawg?"
"No, Jake, but I think you do. I got some things to do. Joan, can you drop my brother off? He only lives a few blocks away."
"I'll take care of your brother. Pop should be around soon. Jake, can you stick around awhile?"
"Sure can. I'll be fine, Dawg. If you stop and see mom before heading out, let her know that I will be home late."

"I'll stop in and let her know. Nice to meet you, Joan." "Same here Aaron, or should I say, Dawg?"
"You can call me anything you want, but call me."
Jake turned to give Aaron the rival stare and said, *"I think she already has your number, Dawg."*

Aaron grinned, gave Joan an affectionate nod, and headed out. The conversation took an unexpected turn for Jake, as Joan began to learn more about Aaron than himself. Jake felt like he was being interrogated as a witness about his brother's character. Each time that he tried to change the subject, Joan inserted a new question about Aaron. Then Jake realized that he was the one being tested. Was he the jealous brother? As the conversation continued, Jerry arrived.

"Hi Jake. I see you have met my beautiful daughter."
"Hi boss. Have a seat."
"Hi pop. Jake and I have been getting acquainted."
"I know how that goes. Is she giving you the third degree?"

Jake sensed that the father-daughter relationship went deep. He knew her pretty well.

"Does she always probe like this?"
"You bet. That's her job, Jake."
"Is she some kind of cop, boss?" Jake said with a smile.
"Second precinct. She's the best officer they have."

Jake's jaw seemed to drop. The heels and leather skirt was a far cry from dress blues, cuffs and a gun. Suddenly, the barrage of questions that he had been answering made sense. He began to think that she gave him the potential felon scan from the bar stool, with the focus on his tattoo. She knew what it meant. Did she come over to probe a suspect as if Jake had committed a crime?

"That explains a lot, boss. Does she give you the hundred questions as well?"
"Used to. Now all she does is give me the look. I become an open book to her after that."
"The look, huh? I better learn what that is."

Joan focused a blank stare towards her father. *"That's it, Jake. That's it. It goes right through you."*

The rest of the evening was filled with humorous accounts of Joan's childhood. There seemed to be a love-hate relationship between a father and his daughter. Jake could sense some pent up emotions regarding her mother's death, but also forgiveness. With each story her father told, Joan took control of the final outcome. She definitely wore the pants in that family.

Marriage Number Two

By the time Jake turned twenty-one, he had spent four months in a federal prison for gun possession, with a rap sheet much longer as a juvenile. A tattoo of a ball and chain was on his right ankle as a symbol of honor and respect from inmates. Prison had instilled fearlessness in Jake that would make anyone back away if provoked. Joan was a police officer who seemed to be drawn to Jake's strengths. Perhaps, she felt she could keep him under control. Perhaps, the attraction was power. Here was a man who could be thrown into prison for any act of abuse. She represented the law.

Jake needed a place to fall and Joan was it. They fulfilled physical needs for each other and were married when he turned twenty-one, after he no longer reported to his parole officer. He stayed straight working as a plumber's helper. The pay was better than minimum wage, but sufficient. Joan's work paid the bills anyway. The road to a productive life was set before him, especially at the birth of their first child, a daughter named Nicole. Jake was present in the delivery room when Nicole was born, and it was an awesome experience. It was a high that he had never experienced before, much higher than the fires in Hawaii and Virginia. He had fathered a child. She was beautiful beyond words.

The relationship between Joan and Jake was like an ocean's surf. At times it was calm. Then the waves began to develop. Joan often brought her work home, affecting both her relationship with her husband and child. Joan served and protected in her job, but Jake became Nicole's protector at home. Often he would take Nicole outside for a swing or a stroll to keep her away from mom's venting. By evening, after Nicole was in bed, Joan's anger control switch was turned off and passionate lovemaking was flipped on. At times the waves reached tidal wave heights, causing Jake to lose control as well. His love for his daughter always brought him back down to reality.

Then another blue-eyed little girl named Alicia was born. The role of fatherhood took on new meaning. His mother played a role in caring for Nicole during those times when both Joan and Jake were at work, but caring for two would have been difficult. Jake decided to limit the time that he would work and stay home with the children. Jerry understood and would use him on tough jobs when Joan was not working. He also enjoyed his role as a grandfather.

Joan began to lose the control that she had over Jake. Somehow, the children became the one's who pulled his strings. The seas were rarely calm in the family and especially the marital relationship. Joan would stay out late without notice almost routinely. Headaches and tiredness filled those times when she was home. He questioned her about her whereabouts without receiving reasonable answers. To say that the marriage was in trouble would be a gross understatement.

> *"You could call when you are not coming home."* Jake would often comment.
> *"Yeah! Well you can leave if you don't like it."*
> *"The kids need a mother."*
> *"They also need a father." "They got that."*
> *"Yeah! They have a convicted felon."* Joan would use his past against him quite regularly.
> *"You're a mother and a police officer, Joan. You have two jobs."*
> *"I'm sick of you Jake. I want you to leave."*
> *"Fine, I will take the kids and move back with mom."*
> *"Yeah! You have turned into a mama's boy."*
> *"I would love to duke it out with you, Joan, but that is not what these kids need. They need a mother and a father. Besides, you would probably have me thrown into the pen for striking an officer."*
> *"Get out, Jake. The kids stay with me."*

The marriage lasted five years. Jake went back to work for Jerry full time, so he kept a relationship with the grandfather of his children, though they lived with their mother and a day care center. Jake tried to gain custody, but the courts sided with Joan. She was both a mother and an officer of the law. He was a convicted felon. It was a no win situation. In addition, he took cash from his weekly pay and gave it to Joan as the court assigned child support. At least he could see Nicole and Alicia during the drop-off. He also received visitation rights, which allowed his ex-wife to follow other desires.

Nicole and Alicia became an intimate part of Jake's life. He relished every moment that he could spend with them. At the same time, he questioned his abilities as a father. The father he knew walked out, and now he was outside the home of his children. He wanted them to always understand that he loved them and would never leave them. If he could, he would snatch them away from their mother. He noticed some bruising at times, but Joan would pass it on as normal child play wounds.

During the first year of their separation, Jake would drop off Nicole and Alicia on a Sunday evening after they had spent the weekend with their father. On some occasions, Joan would seem warm and friendly, causing him to be hopeful of reconciliation. Then came other times when Joan snatched the children away and slammed the door. Her "Jeckle and Hyde" flip-flopping was always a deep concern on his heart. He had a genuine fear for the welfare of his children. In time, any hope for a normal family life for Nicole and Alicia waned. His desire was to let his children know that they always had a safe place to fall, even at their young ages.

Aaron made a few trips to see his parents, while Jake was staying there. Their discussions around the dinner table started from work or sports, but always ended up with the children.

> *"So Jake, when do you get the kids again?"*
> *"Joan's bringing them here Friday evening. I plan on taking them to the zoo on Saturday."*
> *"The zoo, huh? You trying to keep them close to your side of the family?"* Aaron grinned.
> *"No, Dawg. I want them to see your side behind the cages."* Jake returned the rivalry.
> *"You gonna have them all weekend, then?"*
> *"I hope so. That's the plan, anyway."*

"You're going to make a great father someday."
"Maybe, someday." Jake replied. *"I love those kids."*
"I'll tell you something just between us, Jake. They love you too.
I've seen it. Trust me."

Jake pondered those words. At the time, he did not know how Aaron could know that Nicole and Alicia loved him, as they were so young. Yet, there was something in Aaron's voice that indicated the words he spoke had an element of truth. Aaron had not seen Jake that often alone with his children, so his message carried a level of doubt on Jake's part. Still, any reinforcement that he was performing his fatherly role in some admirable manner was gratefully received.

When the divorce was final, Nicole was four and Alicia two. Somehow, Jake would not abandon his children like his father did. These thoughts consumed him. Working for Jerry was a blessing and a curse. The work kept him focused on daily accomplishments, which helped to ease his emotional pain. At the same time, Jerry kept him informed on the events of his ex-wife's home.

"My daughter should have stuck it out with you, Jake. Those
kids are getting a bum rap."
"What do you mean, boss?"
"I think she's got a new beau. Nicole is sent to her room a lot."
"She tells me that, too. When I take the kids back to their
mother, Nicole has a hard time letting go of me."
"You have been a great father to those kids. They idolize you."

Jerry's words struck a heart chord. Jake often doubted his ability to be a good father. His children were the most important things in his life. He truly loved them. He recalled Johnny's discussion about having a purpose in life, and told himself that his purpose was to be a father to these children. The marriage was over, but the relationship between Jake and his kids would not end. He would visit them as often as the courts would allow, and try to be the best dad that he could be. They were everything to him.

A New Relationship

Friday night discussions at the local tavern also ceased, as Jake could not think of anything but the prospect of a leather skirt coming through the door at any time. It would be hard enough to deal with the past baggage of married life, but to know that his children were under someone else's care was heart-wrenching. Various rumors indicated that Joan was already involved with another man. Jake had also known that Aaron had an interest in seeing his ex-wife in more than a social manner. The two brothers had several discussions to that end.

"You don't mind me seeing your ex, do you, bro?"
"Hey Dawg. You do want you need to do. She is not my problem
any more, but those are my kids."
"I'll watch their back. You got my word."
"You need to watch your back, Dawg. She can be meaner than
a junkyard dog, if you know what I mean."
"I'll keep my guard up."
"Just remember. You heard it from me first."

Jake returned to live with his parents for a brief while until he could find a place of his own. A small family restaurant about a block from his apartment became his hangout. Breakfast was pretty reasonable and a cute blonde worked the tables. His loss of a wife did not cause his male hormones to take a break, but there was something about Terry that also touched his softer side. At times, he would come into the restaurant and greet Terry with a warm smile, only to see pain in her eyes.

"What's wrong, Terry?"
"I'm just having a bad week. What can I get for you, sir?"

"Call me Jake, and I'll start with black coffee."
"I'll be right back to get your order, Jake."

After Terry returned, Jake asked about her week. There was something in his smile that seemed to melt away some of her lines of tension. It was as if she wanted a safe shoulder to cry on. Her husband was abusive and had multiple adulterous affairs. She had two children, a boy and a girl about the same ages as Nicole and Alicia, who were being watched by her parents while she eked out a living. Over the next several weeks, Terry would sit down with him whenever business was slow. The discussions would continue after Jake finished work.

"So Terry, did you think about what we talked about this morning?"
"I did Jake. Moving in with you, while I go through my divorce, might prevent me from gaining full custody of my children. I am not sure that I want to take that chance."
"But, didn't you tell me that your husband doesn't want anything to do with the kids."
"I did, but then there's the child support issue."
"That settles it then. You're moving in with me. Even if that idiot doesn't support his kids, I will. What do you say? You don't even have to work as I can pay the bills."
"Well. Sounds like an answer to my prayers."
"Do you pray a lot, Terry?"
"Only when I have no other options. That seems to be all the time now, well …until you came along. I am not that religious, but I can't see how a prayer now and then can hurt."
"I have been reading the Bible, but still have a lot of unanswered questions. I don't think we came here by chance. Maybe, we came from another planet."
"All I know, Jake, is that I can sure use some help."

Terry's husband waged a bitter divorce battle. Moving in with Jake may not have been her best decision, but the demonstrated love Jake had for her children made it worthwhile. Besides, she was able to stay home and nurture them in a calm environment. The pressure of the divorce proceedings was taking a heavy toll. She began attending a Baptist church in her town to find some relief. Jake joined her as he sensed the need to be a better father. Church families, at least on the outside, seemed to have things together when it came to a quality family life.

The members of the church began to counsel Terry about leaving Jake and working to fix her marriage. They told her that any break-up in the family would not be good. She listened intently, as she wanted what was best for the kids, even if the marriage could not be saved. It sounded so cold. She would have to leave Jake. They could no longer live together.

Jake arrived home one evening to find a Dear John note. All of Terry's belongings were gone. The apartment was empty and lonely. The note said she loved him, but was someone else's wife. He felt a rage that he had not felt since his days in the gangs. It rivaled his feelings when his father walked out as a child. God and church became a sudden obstacle. Things seemed to be going so well, and just as quickly, the bottom dropped out.

He went to the minister to plead his case.

> *"What have you done with my woman?"*
> *"Calm down, Jake. You are making a scene here."*
> *"Don't tell me to calm down. Where is Terry? I can't live without her and those kids in my life."*
> *"Come into my office. We can talk there without interruptions."*
> He said this, because Jake's outrage was scaring the other people there.
> *"What lies have you filled Terry's head with, pastor?"*
> *"Try to calm down. If it is God's will for you two to be together, it will happen. You must be patient."*
> *"You want me to be patient,"* Jake screamed. *"The one person in my life who helps he to be patient has just left."*
> *"I understand that you feel hurt. Sometimes, we have to go through times of pain to get new life, like a new mother giving birth."*
> *"So what I am feeling right now is birthing pains? That's a laugh, pastor."*
> *"You need to calm down, Jake. Even if Terry came back now, you need to act rationally, or you will lose her forever. I know you are hurt. It was not an easy decision for Terry as well."*

"I am more than hurt. I'm ticked."

"See, that's exactly what I am talking about. You need to be patient and let God work things out. Do you believe that God exists, Jake?"

"God is someone we imagine when we cannot fix things ourselves. That's what I believe, sir."

"Let me ask you something. Did you see any of your children being born?"

"Nicole and Alicia. I saw them both leave the womb."

"What did you feel at the time?"

"What do you mean?"

"I mean, what was going on inside you when they first entered the world?"

"I heard Nicole's cry and felt an unbelievable joy inside. Is that what you mean?"

"Yes, Jake. Was it a joy that you have ever felt before or since?"

"It was beyond anything I can even imagine. It was an all time high."

"So, Jake. Where do you think that feeling came? You said that it was not experienced before."

"I don't know, but it was real."

"Your body is filled with unexplainable things from a worldly understanding. Have you ever felt a rush of adrenalin?"

"Many times, like the fire in Hawaii."

"The fire, Jake?"

"Yeah! I was in big trouble for starting it, but I felt powerful for some reason."

"Jake, the human body is an amazing thing. A hundred pound woman can suddenly lift a car off of her child during a moment of fear. That's power."

"I can't imagine that."

"It's true. I need you to understand that we are no accident. We are not on this earth by accident, either."

"Wow! Now that's deep, pastor. Johnny and I did some Bible studying together in the pen and he says that we are here for a purpose as well."

Jake seemed to escape for a moment to reflect on Johnny's last words before he went to live with his mother. He was on a mission to discover what his purpose was. He had calmed down before leaving the pastor's office, but the idea of living apart from Terry still troubled him. Later that day, she met him to assure him that she stilled loved him.

> *"Jake. I love you with all of my heart, but we can't live together as long as I am still married."*
> *"I love you too. I can't think of life without you or the kids."*
> *"It won't be that long. All areas of reconciliation have been exhausted. He won't even return my calls. The divorce agreement is nearly complete."*
> *"He's probably with someone else, already. You don't need that abuse anymore."*

They both moved out of the apartment and in with friends. The weeks turned to months, and finally, the divorce was finalized. Three days later they were married by a Justice of the Peace and moved back in together. Terry knew that marrying an unbeliever would not be well received by the church, but she was not willing to live without Jake in her life. They started attending a different Baptist church. Every week, Jake thought that the pastor was talking directly to him. The joy on Terry's face was also infectious.

> *"Pastor Chuck. Your message was directed at me, wasn't it?"*
> *"I don't know anything about you, Jake, except your name. If you felt like the message was personal, then it was, but God was speaking to your heart."*
> *"I want to know more about this God."*

For the next several weeks, Jake's heart was softened. Terry had committed her life to Jesus Christ two weeks after they were married and was baptized. Not only had Jake heard sermons that pierced his heart, but also he witnessed the changes in Terry. Her scales of bitterness were gone, despite the bitter divorce. Something had changed her from the inside and he wanted that change for himself. A month into their marriage and he asked Christ into his life. He was baptized as well.

Jake began to learn what it meant to be a man, a husband, and a father. There is no "i" in any of those responsibilities. God had begun His changing work. He was a changed man. Terry knew that this husband was God's plan for her life as well. Jake agreed to adopt both children and loved them as his own. The road they were on was leading towards an unknown that would be an adventure. Discovering God's plans for them became a daily source of joy.

FAITH AT WORK

Working for Jerry now offered some serious downfalls. Jake needed a new start. Nicole and Alicia were still heavy on his heart. Seeing Jerry on a daily basis only brought thoughts of mistreatment by his ex-wife into his mind. He longed to share his new walk with Jesus with Nicole and Alicia. Having them on weekends was crucial. He did not want to do or say anything that might jeopardize that. Working for Jerry might provide a wrong word or action, so he gave his notice.

Jake now had worked in the plumbing business for five years. He knew a lot of people and had a great reputation. Starting a business was a scary thought, especially without a plumbing license. Yet, that is exactly what he did. A five year old pickup truck with an extended cab was purchased to replace Jerry's company van. On the side of both front doors was a decal of three crosses and Calvary Plumbing was opened for business. Customers called before business cards were even printed, due to word of mouth from previous clients. Jerry may have contributed a bit as well, since he could not handle everything alone. Each month the bills were paid. The idea of making an honest living now sounded great in comparison to the fast money life he knew as a teenager in drugs.

Many jobs that he quoted required a plumber's license to complete, at least legally. Jerry knew that and offered assistance. Though Jake would do the work, Jerry would give the final inspection as well as pass many jobs his way. It was a strange relationship to be sure, but Jerry insisted on staying close. Besides, he was ready to retire, and this provided a momentary bridge. He was confident in Jake's work.

The idea of tithing was also discussed with Terry, and they both agreed it was the right thing to do. After the first month, Jake looked at the income he had received and wrote the check for at least ten percent. Often there was little or no money left in the account after the check was written, but they had faith that God would provide. The money was always there, along with a true sense of peace that it would be. There was always enough for a family vacation, a night out as a couple, or something to help a friend.

Jake often wore shorts when he worked for Jerry, but the tattoo on his ankle was a constant reminder of who he was before. Below the ball and chain was his inmate number. It was no longer a mark of strength, but an embarrassment. Working on his own as a new child of God, meant wearing long pants to avoid displaying the sign of a past life without Christ. The idea of having the tattoo removed or replaced with a new one was constantly on his mind. A new tattoo would have to represent his new life. He was ashamed of his past, but he was not ashamed of the one who gave him new life.

He also knew that he needed Christian men in his life to hold him accountable, lift him and his family up in prayer, and befriend him. He knew that he needed to break out his Bible and study regularly. Through an acquaintance, Jake was introduced into a men's Bible study in another church in the area. He was always amazed how God was leading, first, through Judge Carter. Then they were led to a different church where Jake was converted and baptized. Now, he is visiting another church for a Bible study. The process seemed surreal, but he felt it was God's leading.

Paul was a member of the church where the men's group met. He was leading the study and remembered the first day that Jake attended. Introductions were made and Jake was not shy about sharing his newfound faith. He was a breath of fresh air for Paul. Jake's first impression was awe-inspiring. "Holy cow. This man has a testimony. What a testimony." Paul's study involved getting men to open up and share about the issues bottled up inside them. Until Jake appeared, that task was difficult. The experiences that he shared opened up a floodgate of conversations from the other men. He was like a catalyst and an answer to Paul's prayer for the group. God had placed Jake in that fellowship, not only for his own needs, but also for the rest of the men, especially Paul.

The fire that burns inside a new convert's heart does not go out quickly. Jake demonstrated a love and gratitude for his Lord and Savior that was infectious. He told the group about the desire of his heart to live the Christian life and be held accountable for his actions. He earnestly desired prayer for his new family, his business, and for his daughters. Paul also had his own business in a similar field. He installed water purification systems. At times the two would exchange potential leads for new work. Paul and Jake became great friends, prayer warriors, and accountability partners. Jake's newfound faith was an inspiration to Paul as well.

The biggest problem in Jake's new life was doubt, specifically self-doubt. Perhaps, his past failures or his search for self-gratification became stumbling blocks. The lack of demonstrated love as a child from his father may have instilled disbelief. Then again, it could have been the overwhelming guilt that he held inside for the life he led in his past. Whatever the reason, Paul desired to be Jake's encourager. Paul talked with him at length about the concepts of love and forgiveness.

> *"Jake, do you know how to forgive?"*
> *"What do you mean, Paul?"*
> *"I mean, has anyone ever done something wrong towards you and asked for forgiveness?"*
> *"Nicole, once. It startled me." "So what did you do?"*
> *"I just reached out and hugged her."*
> *"So how did that make her feel?"*
> *"Good, I guess. She stopped crying, anyway."*
> *"Do you remember why she thought she needed forgiveness?"*
> *"Not really. It was something about a broken toy that I bought for her."*
> *"That's interesting. She received your forgiveness through a hug, and yet you don't even know you were giving it. When we ask our heavenly father for forgiveness, He does likewise."*
> *"I don't understand what you mean, Paul."*
> *"Jake, you are hanging on to the guilt of your past sins. Guns, drugs, alcohol, and a riotous life have kept you from having a true relationship with God. You need to confess these things and ask for forgiveness."*
> *"God knows that I have been pretty bad already."*

"That's true, but, He needs to hear you admit to such behavior and ask for forgiveness like Nicole did to you. The beauty of this is that He will forgive you and remove the sins from your account. It is as if they never existed at all. Isn't that what you want my friend?"
"More than anything, friend. More than anything."
"There's something else that I have learned about forgiveness, that you should know."
"What's that?"
"When we harbor ill-feelings in our hearts, God's love doesn't have a place to come in. When people hurt us and we keep a grudge, it can consume us. Forgiving others, including ourselves, is an act of cleansing."
"I never thought of it like that, Paul."

The two men would have many similar conversations over the years, and their faith grew. They encouraged each other regularly. Sunday mornings, Wednesday nights and Thursday night Bible studies became part of their regular meeting times. Both men understood the significance of having good Christian friends. Trying to stay isolated as a believer is not only against the will of God, but may also be a stumbling block for someone else that needs companionship. The spiritual dimension in both men's lives began to grow deeper over the years.

Humans are relational beings. Jake knew that through the love and nurture from his wife and children. He also knew that it would be so easy to be distracted as a man, during the everyday problems with work or home life. The problems that seem unique to us may be commonplace when shared with others. The feelings that we have of being alone quickly pass, when we listen to others going through similar events. Sharing together as men became a part of Paul and Jake's weekly life. Sharing our concerns daily with our father in heaven was also a daily need, which these men learned.

They also learned that it was good to involve others with a passion for Christ. Prayer warriors were only a phone call away at times, and some amazing things were seen as a result. On one occasion, two men in the men's Bible study had asked for prayer for months over the same issue. Each

Thursday evening, they came with the burdens still heavy on their heart. An old friend of Paul's had been part of the group before Jake arrived, but had since moved to another state. Paul called him to ask for prayer one Sunday afternoon.

> *"Hey, friend. What are you doing?"*
> *"Hi Paul. I'm driving to Memphis to teach a class for my company. What's up?"*
> *"Remember the Thursday night men's group?"*
> *"Sure I do, Paul."*
> *"There are two men in the group who have been asking for prayer for a long time, as much as a year now. When I ask you to pray for work for me, the phone starts ringing. I think you have a direct connection."*
> *"I have the same connection as you do. Of course I will pray for these men."*
> *"Chuck's wife has been bed ridden due to a chronic back pain for nearly a year now. When he comes in now, I can see the anguish in his face. Please pray for his wife."*
> *"I will. What is the other concern?"*
> *"Jeff's sixteen-year-old daughter has been in rebellion against her father after her mother's suicide seven months ago. Jeff grieves over the loss of his wife, but is even more heart-broken over the loss of his daughter. Pray for their relationship to draw close."*
> *"Will do my friend, as soon as we hang up. So how are things with you?*
> *"Business is steady but I could always use more."*
> *"I'll pray for your business as well."*

It was about two P.M. when the call ended. Then came another call around the same time the following Friday.

> *"Hey, again."*
> *"Hi Paul. What's happening?"*
> *"Are you driving?"*
> *"Yeah! I'm on the way back home from Memphis. It was a great class. I got to play some golf as well."*

"You better pull over."

"I'm OK, Paul. There's hardly anyone on the road."

"I still think you need to pull off he road."

"What's up? You sound different." "Remember Jeff?"

"The man with the rebellious daughter who lost his wife to suicide?"

"That's the man. Last night we had our study and Jeff came in excited. His daughter met some Young Life teens during the week. She recommitted her life to Jesus and came home this week to seek forgiveness from her father. Jeff was on a cloud. It was beautiful to watch. I told him that I asked for additional prayer after last week's meeting. You should have seen his face."

"You're right. I need to pull over, at least to get the golf towel on my bag to dry my tears. That's great news, Paul."

"That's not all. Are you pulled over yet?"

"I'm on an off ramp. Go ahead."

"Chuck came in last night uplifted as well. His wife was up and walking."

"Wow! Isn't God great."

"You bet. I also told Chuck that you were praying for his wife. He asked when I made the call. I said it was about two last Sunday afternoon. You would have thought he had seen a ghost."

"Why?"

"He checked his wife around one forty-five. She was in such excruciating pain that he went out to the local drug store to find some stronger over–the-counter medicine. When he returned, she was making something to eat in the kitchen. I'm telling you, man. You have a direct connection."

"Right now that connection is to a box of tissues. That's amazing. What a joy to see God at work."

The more stories like these are shared, the greater the faith. Jake had been brought to a Bible study to get into the Word with Christian men and get at least one accountability partner. His prayers were answered. He witnessed first-hand the God of his salvation at work. He knew the power of prayer and how it could sustain him in his life. He had begun to understand the words in Ephesians that insisted there was a God- given purpose for his life. He understood the fellowship of Christian men was a totally different experience than the gang mentality of his youth. He was also being used to minister to Paul.

> *"Hi Paul. How's the water business?"*
> *"Slow Jake, but I'm doing all right. I could use another great month like January, however."*
> *"I know what you mean. My plumbing business has been off as well. Must be the times, huh?"*
> *"The economy is not good right now, but people still need water."*
> *"Friday is the end of the month. I wrote my tithe check and deposited it on Sunday, but I need some jobs to ensure the money is in the bank."*
> *"You mean to tell me that you write checks without the money being there. That sounds pretty foolish."*
> *"I have been doing that for months, Paul, and the deposits are always made in time."*
> *"I applaud your faith in God's promise to provide, but there's a fine line between faith and foolishness. Make sure as you trust God that you are also a wise steward."*
> *"Pray for my business anyway, Paul, and I will ask for customers for you as well. We have to stick together."*
> *"You got it. I'll also call my prayer partner out of state."*
> *"Good. Tell him that I am trying to close a four-month deal on some townhouses. Competition is seriously undercutting the effort."*

Paul made the call soon after Jake left.

> *"Hey, friend. You busy?"*
> *"Not for you, Paul. What's up?"*
> *"I need you to lift up my friend, Jake's, business. He's the plumber that I talked about."*
> *"I remember Jake. What does he need?"*
> *"He's trying to win a large townhouse contract. He has a meeting at two-thirty and is nervous."*

"I will pray that he gets the award and keeps his cool. How's that?"

"Great. I will let you know what happens."

Paul was learning something about faith and the power of prayer as well. Jake won the large job and felt amazingly calm during the meeting. He shared that with Paul.

"Hey, Paul. My prayers have been answered."

"You got the job, Jake?"

"My competition pointed out a major mistake in the last installation that needs correcting and tried to use that to weasel in with his bid."

"What was the problem?"

"I ordered the right conduit for the job, but the supplier delivered the wrong schedule number. I didn't catch it in time. Anyway, it will cost me some bucks to replace the piping."

"So did your competition get the work?"

"No. That's what's so amazing. The owners didn't like the guy. He came across so insincere. I agreed to make the corrections and they awarded me the rest of the units. That's over three months work, Paul."

"That's terrific. I need to call my friend."

"You do that, Paul. But, there's more."

"Okay, I'll bite. What else?"

"The cost of the replacement pipe was not in my account. Out of the blue, the owners asked if I needed an advance to cover some materials. You should have been there. I think my jaw dropped to the floor."

"You're right, Jake. I should have been there. Isn't it amazing how God answers our prayer with even more abundance."

"It sure is my friend. I thought that I had such strength as a foolish teenager, but nothing like what I receive from my Savior. Tell your friend thanks and to keep praying for me."

"Yeah! I ask for his prayers for my business and family as well."

Jake and Paul are growing in their faith. Each time either one experiences God's work in their lives, both are encouraged. They understand that they need each other.

153

A NEW TWIST

Jake enjoyed a new strength with his new family, faith, and friends. The pressures of the plumbing business during a down economy could have taken their toll, but Jake had an inner peace that everything would work out. Spending time with his new family each night was like a dangling carrot to a hungry rabbit. His wife would greet him with a warm embrace when he came home as if to say, "Everything is just fine and I love you." The time he spent with their children also warmed his wife's heart. For the first time, he was experiencing what love really meant. He was being the loving husband and parent, which he had not learned from his father.

Friday nights added his two daughters to the family, as Jake would stop by his ex-wife's home to take them for the weekend. Typically, he would leave an envelope with support monies, load a couple of small suitcases, and bring his children home for two nights. Nicole and Alicia would greet their dad with a warm smile and exuberant embrace. The kids were excited to be with their dad, and Joan was anxious for them to get out of her hair for a while. Things appeared to be working out. At least Jake got to spend quality time with his daughters on a regular basis.

One Friday evening, Jake pulled into Joan's driveway and saw Aaron's truck parked along the road. When he knocked at the door, Nicole and Alicia did not make their usual run to leap on their father. He would brace himself for the onslaught as a precaution. This night Aaron answered.

"Hey, brother."
"Dawg. What are you doing here?"
"I live here. I still have some things to get from my place, but we got married last Saturday."

"Married? I didn't know you guys were an item. Anyway, I wish you both well."
"Thanks bro."
"Are Nicole and Alicia ready?"
"Not tonight, Jake. I need time with them and weekends are my only free moments. We're going to take a trip to the mountains today."
"What! How can she do this to me? She knows they are my kids too."
"Yeah, well, we haven't had a lot of time to discuss the matter. This week has been a blur since the wedding."
"How come you didn't invite me, Dawg?"
"It was a Justice of the Peace thing. Two witness s and about ten minutes was all it took."
"This is not like you, Dawg. You never do things on such a whim."
"I did when we first met. I saved your butt from a thrashing. Don't you remember?"
"I guess I forgot about that day. Since you have been in our house, we discussed things."
"Not everything, Jake. Not everything." "Let me talk to Joan."
"I'll get her. Wait here."

Jake stood just inside the front door. Nicole and Alicia were not in sight and the living room was cluttered with boxes from Aaron's apartment. There were several empty beer bottles on the coffee table, which did not set well inside Jake. The thoughts of his children being exposed to alcohol and a new father figure weighed heavy on his heart. He felt a new form of abandonment. This time his children were being kept from him. Then Joan entered the room. She looked like she just woke up.

"Aaron said that you want to talk to me, Jake?"
"Why didn't you let me know of your intentions, before I drove over? You have a phone."
"The girls clothes were packed for the weekend, but Aaron and I made a spur of the moment decision to go to the mountains. He needs to spend time with them too."
"But, this is my time. I am their father."

> *"You better calm down, Jake, or you'll never spend time with them."*
>
> *"Are you threatening me, Joan? What right do you have keeping my daughters from me?"*
>
> *"In case you forgot, I am their guardian. The court awarded them to me. You get visitation rights, but that can change at any time."*
>
> *"Let me see Nicole and Alicia. Who do they want to spend time with?"*
>
> *"I knew you would be upset, Jake, so I told them to stay in their rooms."*
>
> *"Let me talk to them. I'm calm."*
>
> *"No, Jake. Not tonight. I'll call you next week. We're leaving shortly to go to the mountains for the weekend. Now leave."*

He could see that any further confrontation could erupt into something worse. He was upset, but managed to keep his voice down so his daughters would not be alarmed. He wrote a note for them to read on their trip and handed it to Joan.

> *"Give this to Nicole and Alicia to read. At least let them know that their father was here."*

After reading the note, Joan agreed to give it to them. Nicole was now almost nine and Alicia was seven. The note expressed the love of a father. Jake could not be with them that weekend, but he wanted them to know how he felt. He was not the one abandoning them, and they needed to know that he would always be there.

Jake drove home that evening with mixed thoughts and emotions. There was a new player in the game of life, his brother. How would that affect visitation rights in the future? Was this a forewarning of tougher days ahead? Just how sudden was this relationship between Aaron and Joan? These and many more questions arose in his mind during the short ride home. Upon arrival, Terry met him with her usual warm hug, but this time with a look of surprise on her face.

> *"Where's Alicia and Nicole?"*

*"They're not coming. Joan remarried last weekend and they are
spending this time to get better acquainted in a getaway to the
mountains."*
"That was pretty sudden, wasn't it?"
"Not as sudden as who she married."
"Why? Did you know the man?"
"It was Aaron, by adopted brother."
"So, how long has that been going on?"
"I don't know, but I plan on finding out."
*"The kids are going to be pretty sad. All day they talked about
playing with Nicole and Alicia. They really love them."*
*"I know. I thought about that as I drove back. We have such
great kids."*

Terry's heart took a deep sigh, as she pondered those words. Jake had
become the father to her children that she had longed for. That thought
alone solidified their relationship as husband and wife. At the same time,
she sensed the utter anguish that was in her husband's heart. She longed
to help him through the pain. Then the idea of custody arose in their
conversation.

"What does all this mean, Terry?"
"What do you mean, Jake?"
*"I mean, what if Aaron adopts the girls. Does that mean I will
lose visitation rights?"*
*"You would first have to agree to an adoption as their father.
I don't see that happening."*
*"That will never happen. Joan can still use the courts to get the
visitation times reduced, perhaps to just an hour or two per
week. Can she do that?"*
*"I don't know what the courts will do. We just have to have
faith that God is in control."*
"You're so right. I love you so much."

Jake put his arms around his wife and pulled her next to him. For a few
minutes no words needed to be spoken. They shared one another's strengths
and feelings in a gentle caress. The day started out with great expectations,

and now was coming to a close with two heavy hearts of uncertainty. Life had just handed out a setback and his faith was about to be tested.

Monday morning came and Jake stopped by Jerry's business to pick up a few supplies. Jerry would give him some better prices at times, due to his business connections. This time the meeting was more than just business.

> *"Hi Jerry. What do you think about your daughter's remarriage?"*
> *"That's her business. I try and stay out of it. But, I can tell you that it wasn't unexpected."*
> *"Why do you say that?"*
> *"I guess I can tell you some things now that she's not your wife."*
> *"What things, Jerry?"*
> *"Remember when we would have a few drinks after work on Fridays?"*
> *"I remember."*
> *"You would leave early so that you would not have a hangover with your meeting with your parole officer. Anyway, Aaron would show up within minutes after you left. It was as though he waited for you to leave."*
> *"I don't believe this. You mean they were having a thing before we were married."*
> *"They were more than friends, if you know what I mean. But, they didn't hide it after you were married."*
> *"She was cheating on me with my brother?*

This news sent his mind into a tailspin. Not only was his ex-wife cheating on him during their marriage, but also she did it with Aaron. As a police officer, Joan knew how to control situations. She used Jake's felony record as a control mechanism. Then a thought entered his mind that was even more disturbing. Could Nicole or Alicia or both be Aaron's biological children?

It was this thought that would have him waking up in the middle of the night in a cold sweat. Regardless of who was their biological father, he loved them. A part of him wanted to know the truth, while another side desired to keep that hidden forever. He thought about what difference it would make knowing. There was something about the fear of not knowing that began to drive Jake. He decided that the truth needed to be known, but only to him. Nicole and Alicia did not need to know. That, at least, was his reasoning, and he began the process of DNA testing.

He petitioned the courts to get DNA samples analyzed. The process was set in motion and the results came in about a week later. Both girls had the same ninety-nine-point nine percent certainty rating. Jake was indeed their father. The results brought closure to his heart. At least he would not have to deal with the opposite possibilities.

HEARINGS

Nicole and Alicia would not have the kind of relationship with their dad that they had before. Joan would not let them spend the night, and visits were held to a few hours at a time. Jake could take them out for a movie or a meal, but needed to bring them back within a tight window of time. Her police connections would ensure compliance to her demands. She was in total control and she knew it.

Jake petitioned the courts on several occasions to find out what his rights as a parent actually were. Joan had dictated what his rights were in strong rhetoric, but he needed to get it first hand. One judge told him that unless he could prove infidelity during their marriage or some form of child abuse as a mother, the court's hands were tied. Justice favored a mother, especially when the father was an ex-felon. In this case, the mother was also a respected officer of the law. He had two strikes against him.

One judge agreed to hear his petition and summoned all parties to his courtroom. Jak thought about Joan's adulterous behavior as a key to getting his children back, and entered the courtroom with high hopes. Aaron and Joan also were there with a lawyer. Jake found out rather quickly that by representing himself, he had a fool for a client. The judge asked the appropriate questions.

> *"Joan, during your marriage to Jake, did you have an affair with Aaron?"*
> *"I did not."* Joan responded.
> *"Aaron, did you have an affair with Joan, while she was married to your brother, Jake?"*
> *"I did not."* Aaron replied.

Although Jake tried to insert his accusations, they were quickly dispelled. Joan had made it clear to Aaron that lying to the judge meant rewards later. She held the reins in their marriage, as she had done with Jake. Besides, she convinced Aaron that the burden of proof was on Jake, and that he had none. The session was a learning experience for Jake. In the case of dealing with legal issues, he would need legal counsel. He also needed to let go of the things that he could not control and give them to God.

God had led him through a maze to this point. Surely, He would not abandon him in the middle. If there were a way out, then God would need to provide it. The thought of separation from Nicole and Alicia was burning a hole in his heart. His concern for them as their father was heavy. What could they possibly be learning about living a quality life? They were uplifted everyday in his prayers, though the weeks passed without answers. It was as if God was saying, "Patience my child. Trust in me and things will work out."

The months passed with little change. Jake was able to spend a few hours per week with Nicole and Alicia, but his other children were kept isolated. They were saddened by the lack of interaction that they had enjoyed before Aaron came into the picture. Then came a moment of truth, when Aaron called.

> *"Hello Jake. Can we talk?"*
> *"I'm not sure we have much to talk about, Dawg."*
> *"I know that you are pretty upset towards me, but we have to talk."*
> *"About what?"*
> *"About your girls."*
> *"Oh! So now they're my girls, huh?"*
> *"They have always been your girls, Jake. They talk about you all the time. They want to come and live with you. Joan won't let them go as you know."*
> *"She has to have her fingers tight into everything, even you Dawg."*
> *"Not any more. That's what I need to talk to you about. Can we meet someplace?"*
> *"You can come over here, Aaron."*

"I'll be right over."

The sudden change of heart permeated Jake's thoughts. There was something in Aaron's voice that sounded sincere. Was God answering his prayer? Then again, what could he possibly say to Aaron without building up even more animosity? He gathered these and other thoughts and knelt down to give them to God. He had learned to find peace through prayer. In addition, he gave Paul a call as his accountability partner. Paul then asked for prayer from the men's group. The meeting with Aaron would be immersed with prayer.

Aaron arrived moments later. There was hardly enough time to prepare any conscious thoughts. The meeting between them would have to be spontaneous. Before Jake answered the door, he silently asked for God's wisdom.

"Come on in, Dawg."
"Hi Aaron," Terry said with a gentle hug.
"I needed that. Thanks, Terry."
"Have a seat in the living room and I will put on some coffee."
"That would be great, Terry. Thank you."
"So, Dawg, what's happening?"
"I should have listened to you, Jake. You told me once that Joan was a loose cannon. I didn't believe you."
"Now what has she done?"
"I think the stress of her job has changed her. She is not the same woman I married. Speaking of that, we are getting a divorce."
"Life is more than leather skirts and heels isn't it, Dawg? The kind of love you know doesn't last."
"Yeah, well, even the physical attraction has cooled down quite a bit. A few minutes under the sheets does not erase all of the bickering. I see what you guys have here and I would like that as well."
"You came here to tell us that?"
"I came here to tell you to find a way to get your kids away from her. I think she will harm them or even kill them during one of her raging moments. Nicole and Alicia are petrified. They constantly cry and ask to be with you."

"Has she hurt them? The judge told me that I have a case against her if I can prove abuse."
"Right now the abuse is more mental, but the more they cry to be with you, the more I fear that things will turn ugly."

Jake looked down. He could only think about asking God to intervene on Nicole and Alicia's behalf. He knew all about fear, but he could not imagine what was going through their young hearts and minds. He used to face fear head on to get high on the feelings that followed, but the tears began to stream down his face as he thought about his children. If God had been leading him all throughout his life, then why did he marry Joan? Why were these children born under such a relationship?

Then he recalled the conversations with Johnny and the scripture verses highlighted by Judge Carter. If God had intended a useful purpose for his life, then those in his life must be a part. A sudden burden for Aaron's salvation came upon him.

"Dawg, you said that you were envious of my life. You can have what we have. Do you know that?"
"How can I? Things are crumbling all around me."
"I went through what you are going through, brother. I was married to Joan as well. She was always pretty moody, even with me."
"But you found someone, Jake. Terry is a real blessing."
"She is my friend, but what I found, you can find as well. I found Jesus."
"I tried that church stuff before. It just doesn't work for me."
"I'm not talking about a building. Jesus is alive inside me. I talk to him everyday. He wants to be there for you as well."
"I just don't know what to think. I wish there were someone like Terry out there for me as well."
"Why don't you come to church with us on Sunday. Maybe you can meet someone there."
"I thought you said it wasn't about a building."
"Its not, Dawg. It's about relationships. I want you to find the kind of relationship that I have, not only with my new family,

but also with my Savior. When I was barely a teenager, you were my savior. I would have taken a severe beating, remember?"
"The odds were a bit against you."
"But you stepped in to help me, and I never forgot it. You were a perfect stranger, yet you risked your own life to help me. I have learned that through our rebellion, we became strangers to the God who created us. Jesus came to reconcile us with the Father by giving His own life as a ransom. I know that doesn't make a lot of sense now. It didn't for me at first either. Come to church with us. Please come, Aaron."

It had been many years since Jake called him by his real name, Aaron. The term "Dawg" had taken root, but there was something in hearing the name, "Aaron" that struck a chord like nothing ever heard before. It was personal and at the same time loving. Aaron came to that house to alert Jake about the impending peril that he sensed for Nicole and Alicia. He had done that, but now felt relief for the pain of self-doubt welled up inside him.

"I'll be there. I will see you in church on Sunday. I only hope that the walls don't cave in from the shock." Aaron smirked.
"I felt that way the first time too, bro. The walls are strong." Jake returned the smile.

Sunday morning came and Jake wondered if Aaron would keep his word and show up. Jake would come early with his family for various Bible study classes, so they did not expect him until the service that followed afterwards. Prior to the start of the classes, the adults could gather at a small café area with tables. Coffee and refreshments were available. He enjoyed that time of social interaction. This was a Sunday that he would not forget. During the week, Aaron stopped by the church office to get the information regarding worship times and events. He met with the pastor and openly discussed the events of the past week. In the process he asked Jesus into his heart. Jake did not know about what had transpired. He just looked at Aaron as he came into that café section that morning.

"You're here already. I didn't expect you until eleven when the service starts."

"Yeah, well, I thought a lot about what you said the other night and checked this place out during the week. I met with your pastor as well."
"Really, did he give you any words of wisdom?" Jake maintained a sheepish grin during the exchange.
"I did it, Jake. I asked Jesus into my heart. I am going to be baptized next week."

You could almost hear a pin drop as Jake moved to embrace his brother. Tears of shear joy streamed down the cheeks of both men. The collision path set before two brothers had changed course to a place of joy and refuge. Jake began to understand so much more about his purpose in life. Whatever bitterness was in his heart over his brother's affair with his wife was now gone. The two men were at peace with each other and now also with God.

NEW EVIDENCE

Although the DNA tests results came as a relief to Jake's heart, he was still troubled by the thought that these girls were being raised without a father. Spending a few hours a week was not enough to compensate for the immoral, and perhaps, controversial training they were receiving from their mother. He was praying fervently for answers. Aaron's words still echoed inside his head, and he feared that Joan might fly off the deep end one day. It was one of his missions in life to get Nicole and Alicia safely away from their mother. He longed to be the father to them, which he had never had. The more he was separated from them, the more inadequate he felt. Without Terry's support, life would have been agonizing to say the least.

As a police officer, Joan knew the outward signs of abuse. If she was physically harming Nicole or Alicia, it was not evident. Bruise marks may have been present somewhere, but Jake never saw them. The idea that she was an abusive mother just did not seem to be a way of getting the children away from her. Jake was emotionally torn as he thought about the mental abuse and possible riotous living that Nicole and Alicia might be exposed to. Still, it was all conjecture on his part. He had nothing concrete to take to the courts.

After Aaron's conversion, while his divorce was being finalized, he moved in with Jake. Above the garage was a bonus room, used as a playroom for the kids. Jake added a bathroom with a shower. To Aaron it was home, and he loved having the children come up to play as well. Jake and Aaron read scripture together and openly shared.

"Hey, Dawg. I need to know something."

"Yeah, Jake. What is it?"

"Why did you lie to the judge about not having an affair with Joan while I was married to her?"

"I guess I was scared, Jake."

"Scared? You mean to tell me that the man who saved me from a thrashing years ago was scared of a hundred and twenty pound woman?"

"She has more power than that whole gang of hoodlums, Jake. She has the law."

"What are you scared of? You were never charged with anything."

"I had my run-ins. A couple of DWIs were swept under the carpet, if you know what I mean."

"She bailed you out, huh?"

"Yeah. Sometimes I was even with her snorting cocaine. She knows more about me than you ever will, bro."

"I guess she threatened you with the juicy stuff, huh? Is that why you lied?"

"That was part of it, but she had a way of manipulating what happened in the bedroom as well. Lying offered the best options if you know what I mean."

"I guess, but your testimony sure hurt any chances that I had to get my girls back."

"I felt bad about it then. You have to believe me. But, since I have come to know Jesus, my heart is more troubled now."

"Jesus will do that to you, but He has your best interests at heart. Trust me."

"I know He does. I know He does. Come upstairs with me. I want to show you something."

The two men went upstairs to Aaron's bedroom. Aaron opened a lower drawer in his dresser and pulled out a packet of envelopes that were banded together. He handed them to Jake.

"I think you need to read some of these."

"What are they, Dawg?"

"Most of them contain letters from Joan while you guys were married."

Jake's eyes became as wide as saucers. Could this be the evidence that he needed to prove to a judge that his wife was unfaithful? Would it be enough to win custody of Nicole and Alicia? These questions and others raced through Jake's mind. He first seemed to stare at the outside of the envelopes without opening them.

> *"Jake, what's wrong? You look like you've seen a ghost or something."*
> *"Why did you keep them?"*
> *"I don't know. I read them over and over when you were married, however. I guess I did not want to let go of her."*
> *"The stamped dates on the outside prove that you were having your affair during my marriage. Surely, the courts will believe me now."*
> *"Do you think it is enough to get your girls back? She is still their mother."*
> *"All I know is what the judge told me. He said that if I could prove infidelity on her part during our marriage, then I had sufficient grounds for an appeal in a custody hearing. These letters may be just that."*
> *"I truly hope they can help. I want those girls away from her as much as you do."*
> *"If I use them in court, will you get in trouble for false testimony?"*
> *"Perhaps, Jake, but don't concern yourself about me. You need to do what is right for those girls."*
> *"Let's pray about it anyway, brother."*

The two men knelt beside Aaron's bed and opened their hearts to the Lord. Hearts were emptied from the burdens they faced and then filled with a new sense of peace. Aaron petitioned for forgiveness for the lies that he had uttered about his affair at the last hearing, and felt God's hand tap him on the shoulder. He knew something about feeling powerful from his teen years, but he was now plugged into a new source much greater than anything he had ever felt before. With it came a peace that was indescribable. It was as if scales of guilt fell off his body, when he felt God's hand tap him.

The power also flowed over to Jake. There was something magical in that quiet time together. Whatever doubts or ill feelings each man had towards each other were removed. They stood up and embraced. Tears streamed down their faces.

> "Dawg. Things are going to work out, I just know it."
> "I know it too, Jake. I sensed God's hand is in whatever happens. I cannot describe the feeling."
> "We need to pray together more, brother."
> "That's the second time today that you called me 'brother'. I like the sound of that."
> "Me, too, brother. Me, too."

Jake took the letters to a quiet place and began to sort through them. He opened one, dated six months after they were married. The words used by Joan described intimacy in x-rated terms. Just reading about where Joan wanted to place her hands on Aaron's body would arouse any man. Surely, these words can be used against her in court. He continued to scan through several other letters with the same lustful intensity coming through loud and clear. He also shared the contents with Terry and they prayed together.

Were these letters the evidence that he needed to get his daughters back? That was the question. This time, Jake would not rely on his own understanding of the law, and he sought proper council. He brought the letters to a lawyer, recommended by one of the members of his church. The lawyer agreed to review his case, read the letters, and get back to him the following week. Jake left the office with mixed emotions as he was told not to get his hopes up too high. His ex-wife's work as a law enforcement officer still had a lot of weight in the judicial system.

The following week's meeting was much more optimistic. The letters were quite revealing to the lawyer as to his ex-wife's character, and certainly merited a new court date. The appeal was filed the following week.

Jake could only reflect upon the events that just happened. The new evidence was an answer to prayer. He had a new and restored love for Aaron. The possibility of getting custody of his girls was now more real than ever. God was definitely at work in his life. He had come a long way in his life. Yet, he still questioned his God-given purpose.

REPERCUSSIONS

Setting up a new court date offered new hope, yet Jake would find out that there are always two sides to a coin. If a boxer strikes a blow, he should expect a counter punch. Joan was not without recourse and would fight back. She filed an additional lawsuit directed against Jake for failure to pay child support. She claimed that she had not received support payments for over six years. Florida laws may not have been as strict as some states, but conviction would still carry harsh penalties, including payment restitution and even jail time.

Jake received a letter from the court system requesting his presence at a hearing two weeks before the custody date. A judgment against him in this suit will certainly lessen any chances of winning his girls back. The custody hearing may even be dismissed with an unfavorable result in Joan's counter suit. He wondered as to what other concealed weapons she would use against him. He had paid her the agreed one hundred dollars a week support, but it was always paid in cash. He would pick the girls up and hand Joan the envelope, usually with five twenty-dollar bills inside

Now he had the burden of proof, as he never used checks. Until starting his plumbing business, banking and checks had no purpose. He would receive a paycheck and pay a service fee to an institution to cash it. His days of dealing in drugs as a teenager taught him that money talks. Clients paid him in hard currency or they did not receive the goods. Terry helped Jake understand the banking industry and how to be a better steward of what they had. Nevertheless, he had continued the habit of paying Joan with cash placed in a plain envelope each week. On a few occasions, he made a double payment, when he knew that he would not be in town the following week. Yet, he had no proof. How could he convince a court system that he was faithful? Joan was an upstanding member of the law.

The back child support monies totaled over thirty thousand dollars. If the courts decided that Jake could avoid jail time by making the payment, his business could not raise the monies. Jake and Terry prayerfully sought God's help on a daily basis. They watched the monies come in at the end of each month to stay afloat. It was part of their spiritual growth. Jake had a business checking account, which Terry helped to manage, so both were well aware of the financial conditions of his business. The same account was used to pay their household bills. Often they would write church tithing checks based on what they felt the Lord wanted them to give, without the monies in the account to support the checks. Yet, they would watch God perform amazing things. Tithing checks would not bounce as either a new client would suddenly appear, or a customer bill would be satisfied at the eleventh hour.

For the next two weeks, Terry and Jake found themselves focused in prayer over the upcoming court date. Although he may have had an outward expression of worry, he was at peace on the inside. He knew that he could rely on God to work one more miracle in his life. Aaron added his prayers as well. Jake tried to keep the news about the lawsuit from him, but Aaron could sense a heavy load on his brother's heart.

> *"Hey Jake! You don't seem to be yourself today. What's up?"*
> *"I'm fine. I just have a lot of things going on that I have to deal with."*
> *"Like what?"*
> *"Things, Dawg. Just things."*
> *"Whatever these 'things' are brother, they must be pretty hard. You look terrible."*
> *"Work is a bit slow right now. You know, things."*
> *"Come on Jake. You have lots of slow days, yet you always seem to be above all that. That's what I love about you. You never seem to worry. Today, I see worry written all over your face. Talk to me."*
> *"It's Joan. She's claiming that I owe her child support."*

"You always pay her. I have seen the money in an envelope after you pick up the girls."
"Do you think that your words can satisfy the judge?"
"I will support you and testify, if that's what you mean?"
"I mean, do you think that any judge would believe you over her? I never asked for a receipt."
"I would hope so. I surely would hope so. At the very least, we can pray about it."
"I have been on my knees specifically over it, but one more petition can not hurt."
"When is the court date?"
"Next Tuesday at eleven in the morning."
"I will be there for you, brother. I will be there."
"Are you sure that you can get off work, Dawg?" (Jake said this with a wry smile, as Aaron was between jobs at the time. Occasionally, he helped Jake in his plumbing business,)

Jake's house had become a place of closeness and prayer. The brother, whom had slept with his ex-wife, had become his close friend. That, in itself, was a miracle. The teenager who saved Jake from a thrashing had been reinstated as a trustworthy companion. There was something in their spiritual journey together that added a new sense of inspiration to their relationship. It was almost surreal.

Tuesday morning came. Jake his family, and Aaron headed out to the courthouse early. Jake was concerned, that if he arrived even one minute late, his case would be over and Joan would win. The courthouse was only a ten-minute drive away, but allowing at least an hour to get there sounded reasonable. After all, a tire may suddenly go flat or an accident may delay the process. He was full of the "What ifs." He was unsure about how the day would turn out, but he knew that God was in control. They arrived without incident and had plenty of time to gather themselves.

As courtroom activities go, the appointment times are more like suggestions. Good judges may be able to control each session to a reasonable time limit, but not always. Cases can be as unpredictable as an infant's cry. When they located the assigned room for the hearing, the door was open and no one was inside. All of the previous cases had either been completed or satisfied through mitigation without a hearing. Jake, Terry, Aaron and the children entered the room and took seats near the front. It was almost eerie. The expected throng of people from other pending cases was missing. The silence was unexpected and welcomed. Together, the family sought the Lord in prayer.

A clock was located on both the front and back walls of the courtroom. The minutes ticked closer and closer to the eleven o'clock hour. Each click sounded like a loud clap. The room remained silent while they waited. Jake kept peering back towards the entry doors, expecting to see Joan come in. Their case was the last one on the judge's agenda before his customary two-hour lunch recess, which explained why other case participants had not entered. Yet, Joan was not there either. Jake began to question, why.

Then a man wearing a business suit entered the room. Jake had learned his lesson and had contacted a lawyer to represent him who was also a member of his church. They had met on the first Sunday after Jake received the summons to appear. Mr. Donaldson had agreed to represent him after discussing the matter over a cup of coffee at the church's coffee shop.

"Hi Mr. Donaldson."
"Hi Jake, but you can call me Andy. Is that okay with you?"
"Sure, Andy. Where is everybody? I expected a throng of people on Joan's side of the room."
"Hearings like this are not like the Perry Mason trials on television, Jake. Usually, only a handful of people show up for child support claims."
"Yeah, but Joan's not here either. It's already past eleven o'clock. I thought waiting like this was reserved for doctors or dentists."
"...or lawyers?" Mr. Donaldson said with a grin.
"Okay. Lawyers, too."
"That is why I am running a bit late as well. I met with Joan's lawyer and the judge earlier."
"Don't tell me that everything is postponed. This is really taking a toll on me, not to mention the work that I am not doing to earn a living."

"Speaking of work, I need to have you come over and give me a quote on replacing some bathroom fixtures. Let me know when you have a moment."

"Anytime, Andy, but, what about this case?"

"Phillip, Joan's lawyer, had a long talk with me last night over the phone. He has convinced his client to drop the suit."

"What do you mean, drop? Will it bounce back at a later date?"

"I mean drop it completely, Jake. Phil does not believe her claims are real. He found several people to collaborate your story. Your children said that they had seen the envelope many times when you picked them up. The suit is closed forever." "I can't believe it. You mean that I fretted for nothing?"

"I mean that you have nothing to fret about. You have been praying over this, haven't you, Jake?"

"Of course. I pray almost continuously. I know that I need to 'let go and let God' work. Is that what just happened here, Andy?"

"Giving God the credit for answered prayers can't hurt. You do that, Jake. You do that."

"You bet I will and I am."

Aaron was also moved by the news. He had wondered about how his testimony would be received and whether it would help Jake's cause. Now that was all a mute point. God had intervened. He reached over and hugged his brother. Without a word being spoken, both men felt joy and an extra measure of peace during the exchange.

"We have such an awesome God, don't you think?"

"Beyond awesome," Jake responded.

Terry joined in the embrace and the tears trickled down each face. God had indeed worked things out.

"So tell me, Andy. Why did Joan break it off? That's not like her."

"She concocted the story out of anger over the summons she received from you. It was a control thing."

"I understand that, but still she never backs down."

"Let me put it to you this way, Jake. If she continued the suit and lost, then she would be seriously discredited in your suit

to get those girls away from her. Phil simply pointed out to her that judges are human and the testimony of your daughters would cast serious doubt on her ability to convince them that you have not paid your child support. Even if you missed payments, she claimed that you had not made any. Do you see her dilemma?"

"I do. Thank you Mr. Donaldson, I mean Andy."

"You're welcome, Jake. It was my pleasure. Now when can you take a look at my fixtures?"

"How about after lunch. Can you join us?"

"I have a busy schedule this afternoon, but this evening would be great. I will pass on lunch, but how about a rain check?"

"You got it, and I will call you after five tonight to look at your bathroom."

"Just come over anytime and bring your whole family. My wife would love to meet you."

This was another one of those defining moments in Jake's life. The day started out with a cloud of doubt and ended with sunshine. He learned that worrying about the future could only cause negative results. Leaving everything in God's hands was a far better option.

THE DOORS OPEN

Jake was unusually nervous at the Thursday night men's Bible study. The weight of the upcoming custody hearing weighed heavy on his heart. The men gathered around, placed their hands on him, and prayed for an extra measure of God's peace. Jake said that he felt that God was in control no matter what happened. The day of the hearing he felt the peace that those men prayed for.

It's now one twenty-five and the courthouse doors are opening. The room was empty, as the two-hour lunch break had ended. The scheduled time for his hearing was two o'clock, so it was time to have a seat. Giving character testimony was not unusual for me. Parole officers are often called in when convicted felons face various proceedings, but this was special. I had seen a man totally change his life over the last ten or twelve years. The man I knew that was incarcerated has been freed from the bondage of his past. Jake was now living a life that I could only dream possible for him. He is truly a loving husband and father. I have not had contact with him since his latest marriage, but I did know Joan while Jake was assigned to me.

Jake gathered his wife and two children and led them into the courtroom to take their places. I waited until they sat down before taking a seat a few rows back. Up to this point he did not see me. If he did, he did not recognize me as his parole officer. The last time we spoke together was about nine or ten years ago. I closed the doors behind me. The room held about eighty people based on the number of seats, but appeared as though it could hold several times that amount. The windows were large to match the vaulted ceiling. Yet, as I took my seat you could hear a pin drop.

The doors opened once again and a man entered dressed like a minister. Jake turned to see who it was, but he did not recognize him. As he turned, however, his eyes looked upon my face.

> *"Mr. Patterson, is that you?"*
>
> *"It is, Jake, but please call me George. How are you doing?"*
>
> *"Don't you mean Harley? Never mind how I am doing. What brings you to my custody hearing?"*
>
> *"Your lawyer asked me to come. I think that he wants me to say a few words about your character. You are a real character, you know."*
>
> *"My lawyer must know what he is doing, at least I trust his judgment. I tried to defend myself in a similar hearing once and had a fool for a client."*
>
> *"You'll do fine today, Jake. Who's the fine looking lady and children with you?"*
>
> *"This is my wife Terry, our son Matt and daughter Diana. Terry has another daughter and we just became grandparents. How about that, George? I'm a Grandpa."*
>
> *"That's terrific. I was watching you guys in the atrium. You seem made for each other."* Terry heard those words and a warm loving smile filled her face.
>
> *"My old ways are gone, George. I have been reborn."*
>
> *"So what have you been doing with your life, Jake?"*
>
> *"I have my own plumbing business and God has blessed me."*
>
> *"I can see that. I remember a different man who came to my office on Saturdays. As I recall, you were working for a plumber then. I guess it paid off, huh?"*
>
> *"A lot has happened since you last saw me, George. A lot."*

The doors opened again and Joan entered with her lawyer. Before she sat down across from Jake, she managed to make eye contact. She still had that look of determination that Jake had always known. Without a single word uttered, he sensed her desire to stay in control of their children and Jake. He offered a greeting, but Joan did not respond.

Others began to enter. By the time the bailiff announced the judge's entry, the room was nearly half full.

"All rise," the bailiff cried out.
"The honorable Judge Anthony Carter presides," he continued.

Jake's chin seemed to drop. Could this be the same judge who sentenced him? Then he remembered the prison visit and the Bible. There was something in the name that brought peace to Jake's heart. Judge Carter was one man who truly turned his life around. He had not seen the judge for many years. He didn't remember his first name as being Anthony, but "Carter" was a welcomed relief. Then a man wearing a robe stepped towards the bench. If he was the judge Jake knew, then he had grown about six inches and put on a lot of extra weight. Jake realized that this man was not the Judge Carter that he knew. Yet, there was still something in that announcement that brought peace to his heart.

"Take your seats," the judge motioned. *The court will now hear the custody case of Wilson vs. Wilson."*

Jake thought about that for a moment. Joan changed her name to his when they were married. She could have reverted back to her maiden name, but then she also married his adopted brother, Aaron. He had his name changed to Wilson in the process. Somehow, it all seemed weird to hear as the judge spoke "Wilson vs. Wilson." Nicole and Alicia had also maintained his name. Judge Carter made his opening remarks.

"Custody hearings are meant to determine what is best for the welfare of the children. This is not a jury trial. I will listen to all testimony prior to making a ruling. Does each party have legal representation?"
"We do," unanimously responded.
"Does Mrs. Wilson have any opening remarks before we get started?"
"We do," her attorney said as he stood.
You have the floor councilor."
"Thank you, your honor. Up to now, Mr. Wilson has had visitation rights on weekends. At times the children return with noticeable anger rages and other symptoms, which we feel are the result of their exposure to their father. In order to keep a more stable environment for Nicole and Alicia, her

mother would like to limit visitation to four hours a week with supervision."

Jake's lawyer had told him to be prepared for some mudslinging and could sense that he wanted to leap up. He pushed down heavily on Jake's thigh as if to say, "Not now." The idea that Jake would have to be supervised when with his children struck a negative chord, not to mention the limited number of hours. He looked around the courtroom to see if Nicole and Alicia were present. They were not. He felt somewhat better as they had not heard the accusations.

"In addition, Judge, we would like the court to raise the child support payment from one hundred dollars a week to two hundred. The children are older and require more expensive clothing, school supplies, and other items. Mr. Wilson has his own business, and we feel can support our request."

The judge did not make an immediate response to the opening statement. He turned to Jake's lawyer and asked for his opening remarks.

"My client, Jake Wilson, adores his children and wants only the best for them. He has seen them exposed to riotous living from their mother as well as heard their desires to come and live with him. He feels that it is in their best interest to be removed from their mother's home and placed in their father's custody. He has proven himself as a loving husband and father in his present marriage, and his wife is equally supportive of the idea. The best interest of Nicole and Alicia is to be separated from their mother and placed in my client's home."

As his lawyer spoke, Joan grimaced. She thrived on power in any relationship, including the marriage to Aaron. Although she kept her cool during the opening statement, inside she was boiling. There was no way that the children would be taken from her, at least in her mind. Judge Carter then addressed the audience.

"The court's concern is for the welfare of these children. As the one who presides over these proceedings, I will make the final decision. I will hear testimony from both sides, beginning with

Mrs. Wilson. The case of Wilson vs. Wilson is now open." He said this for the court stenographer to capture.
Are the children present in this court?" The judge asked.
"They are not, Your Honor. They are with their grandfather. We felt it would be better for them if they were not here," Joan's lawyer replied.
"Let the record show that Nicole and Alicia are not in this courtroom," Judge Carter told the stenographer.

Custody hearings allow each lawyer to question those who testify. In addition, the judge can also question them to get clarity. Unlike a jury trial, the ultimate decision rests with the judge. Body language and attitudes play a big role. Jake received instructions from his attorney to stay calm, but he knew that God was in control. The first witness called was officer Wilson's partner. After he was sworn in, Joan's lawyer started his questioning.

"State your name for the record."
"John Amos."
"What is your connection to this case?"
"Officer Wilson is my partner. I have known her over nine years."
"How do you rate her as a partner?"
"Officer Wilson is a dedicated professional. I trust her with my life."
"Have you ever witnessed Officer Wilson get angry or overstep her authority while on the job?"
"No, sir. I have not."
"Have you ever seen her with her children outside of duty?"
"We have had many outside gatherings with family, like clam bakes, picnics, etc. Officer Wilson insists that these be held at her house so she can be near her children"
"How do you rate her as a mother, based on your observations during those events?"
"Those children mean the world to her. You can tell."
"What do you mean? How can you tell?"
"They are well-behaved. They are very respectful towards their mother. Officer Wilson also leaves the parties early to ensure they get their rest."

"So, Officer Amos, can you tell the court of any reason why Officer Wilson should be considered an unfit mother?"
"No reason. She's a great mother."
"Thank you, Officer Amos."

Jake's attorney stood and walked towards the witness chair.

"Tell me Officer Amos, have you ever had drinks with your partner after work?"
"Occasionally."
"Do you know where Officer Wilson's children are during that time?"
"I think her father watches them or she has a sitter."
"Does Officer Wilson drink alcoholic beverages in front of her children at those so-called outside gatherings with the other officers."
"I can't recall." The judge was quick to notice a nervous twitch during the response.
"Tell me Officer Amos, do you drink alcohol at those gatherings?"
"I have a beer or two, yes."
"Where are Officer Wilson's daughters during those times?"
"I think they are sent to their room." He said this to not place the girls in the presence of alcoholic beverages. Once again, the judge was quick to notice uneasiness.
"Earlier, you told us that the girls were respectful and well-behaved during those events. How do you know, if they were in their room?"
"We would see the girls when we first arrived at Officer Wilson's home."
"I have one last question, Officer Amos. Have you ever been at Officer Wilson's home the morning after one of those gatherings?"
"I have not." The judge sensed a third act of nervousness.
"Thank you Officer Amos."
"I have a question for you Officer," Judge Carter continued.
"Have you ever seen Officer Wilson unfit for duty following one of those gatherings?"

After a long pause, Officer Amos responded,

"No, I have not."

The witness was told to take his seat, while Jake wondered why the judge asked the last question. He reasoned that if Joan was hung over occasionally, then her motherly responsibilities might be affected. If the answer indicated that Joan was unfit for duty, then that might be the case, but the answer did not reflect that she was unfit. Jake was not trained in picking up body language signs, unlike the judge.

Joan's lawyer then called his next witness, one of her neighbors. She was sworn in and took the stand.

"State your name for the record, please."
"Mary Roberts."
"What is your relationship to this case?"
"I am Joan's next door neighbor."
"Why are you here?"
"On many occasions I watch Nicole and Alicia while their mother works, usually after their school lets out. These girls are such a joy, normally."
"What do you mean, normally?"
"When they spend the weekend with their dad they usually return with an attitude that following Monday."
"What do you mean, "attitude"?
"They are very hard to control. They say disrespectful things to me. Their personalities seemed to change into something less desirable, at least as far as I was concerned."
"So, you attribute the changes to time spent with their father?"
"Of course."
"Thank you Mrs. Roberts."

Jake looked upset by the testimony, but remained calm. His lawyer continued to tap him on the thigh to acknowledge that he understood. Jake turned towards his representation and whispered into his ear. Then the lawyer moved towards Mrs. Roberts to cross-examine.

"Tell me Mrs. Roberts, or can I just call you Mary?"
"Mary, would be fine."

"So Mary, have you ever been asked to watched the girls late at night?"

"Sometimes, yes."

"Have they ever spent the night at your house?"

"Occasionally. Usually, I suggest that, when I know Joan has a lot on her plate, especially as a police officer."

"When was the last time those girls spent the night, Mary?"

"I think it was a week ago on Friday."

"What were the circumstances that led to that occasion? I mean, what was Joan doing at the time?"

"She called me about ten or so and said that she was discussing a case with fellow officers, and did not know when the meeting would break up. I suggested that the girls stay the night."

"Would you say that Nicole and Alicia were the well-behaved kids that you described earlier, or disrespectful?"

"Well-behaved for sure. They were little angels. We had a great evening together."

"You testified earlier, that these girls had a marked change in their attitudes after spending time with their father. I have one last question for you, Mary. Could it be possible that their change in behavior was caused by the fact that these girls had such a great time with their father, that they wanted to stay with him?"

"Objection!" Joan's lawyer burst out. *"Any answer would be hearsay."*

Judge Carter sustained the objection and asked Mary to disregard the question. The question was out on the table for everyone to hear. Jake inserted the question into his lawyer's ear, and it left a mark. The girls had repeatedly asked their father if they could stay with him, especially after he had remarried. They felt loved and respected by Terry as well. They felt free to do non-regimented things together and with the other children. The idea that they returned from visitation with their father had brought on some emotional disorder or stress caused by mistreatment had been countered by another possibility.

Throughout the cross-examination process, Joan maintained an intense stare focused directly at Jake. He felt it, but would not return in kind. Up to now, the court proceedings had not brought forth any unexpected trauma for him. He asked God for wisdom and peace prior to entering the room, and God had provided. The contempt in Joan's face painted a different picture.

JOAN'S TESTIMONY

The last witness called by Joan's lawyer was his client. Joan was asked the same question as the others in the swearing in process, but it took on special meaning for Jake.

> *"Do you promise to tell the truth, the whole truth so help you God?"*
>
> *"I do,"* Joan responded.
>
> *"State your name for the record."*
>
> *"Joan Wilson."*
>
> *"Are you the mother of Nicole and Alicia Wilson?"*
>
> *"I am proud to be their mother."*
>
> *"Do you consider yourself to be a good mother, Joan?"*
>
> *"Yes, of course."*
>
> *"Why is that, Mrs. Wilson?"*
>
> *"I provide a home, food, clothing, and a loving environment for my girls."*
>
> *"Do you discipline them?"*
>
> *"I set rules and boundaries along with the consequences. If they step over their bounds, I enforce the rules."*
>
> *"Do you ever strike your children, Mrs. Wilson?"* He asked this question in anticipation of it being asked by opposing council.
>
> *"Once, I slapped Nicole on her mouth for back talking. She had just returned from being with her father and said something disrespectful to me."*
>
> *"Was this a normal occurrence after being with her dad?"*

"Usually, after spending more than a few hours. That is one of the reasons why I am requesting a limited visitation right with supervision."

"I see, Mrs. Wilson. So let me get a clearer picture here. When the girls are with you and not under their father's influence, they adhere to the rules and are well behaved. When they return from having long visits with their father, they have sudden mood swings. Have I got that right, Mrs. Wilson?"

Jake maintained his composure during the summation, although he knew why the mood swings took place.

"That's pretty much the story. These girls need to know their father, but not be nurtured by him. After all, he is a convicted felon."

"Have you ever told these girls that their father had been in prison?"

Once again, he knew this question might come up later and wanted to be the one to bring it up. Jake's lawyer rose with an immediate objection.

"Jake's past, prior to their union, has no relevance."

"Overruled," the judge cried. *"I want to hear her answer."*

"I didn't have to tell them. They knew."

"How would they know without you telling them? Did Jake tell them?"

Jake had a ball-and-chain tattooed on his ankle along with his convict number. They saw it routinely. When they were old enough to ask about it, he told them that he had been a bad man and had to be locked up for a while. They knew that it was before they were born."

"How did Nicole and Alicia react when they heard about his incarceration?"

"Like children. They knew when they would be bad they would be sent to their room."

"Did they understand why their dad was imprisoned?"

"They knew it was over carrying a gun and asked me why I was not in that place when they saw me carrying."

"That must have been strange for you to hear. How did you answer them?"

"I talked about my job as someone who protected people from doing bad things to others. I showed them my badge and discussed my job with them. I told them that you had to have a license to carry a gun and that their daddy did not have one. I told them that anyone who carries a weapon has a huge responsibility. The process of getting a license includes knowing what those responsibilities are."

"Do you really think they understood all that? They must have been pretty young?"

"Perhaps, not at first, but I would bring home newspaper clippings and other photographs of bad people that I arrested. I would show them the difference between my role a police officer and a common criminal with a gun. They may not have understood initially, but I think they do now. Nicole is almost a teenager."

"Objection," Jake's lawyer yelled emphatically. "My client is not to be labeled a bad man for his actions prior to the birth of these children. He paid his debt to society."

"I would like to insert a question to you Mrs. Wilson," Judge Carter insisted. "Do you ever tell your children that your ex-husband, Jake, is a bad person."

The judge was even more watchful of Joan's reaction to his question as he listened for her response.

"I have not, your Honor." (Her expression told a different tale, however.)

"You may continue councilor."

"One last question, Mrs. Wilson. What do you feel would be in the best interest of these children today?"

"I believe that spending unsupervised time with their father would cause far more harm than good. I can provide a nurturing environment that would keep them safe, healthy, and well adapted in this world."

"Your witness councilor."

Before Jake's lawyer approached the witness, he bent down to whisper something to his client. The concern on Jake's face, over the picture Joan had just painted, suddenly seemed to dissipate. Whatever was said had a calming effect. The cross-examination of his ex-wife had been discussed at length, prior to that day.

"*So tell me Mrs. Wilson. How is your relationship with Jake today?*"

"*We don't talk very much. I am always afraid to say something that would provoke him.*" (She said this to further her claim that he was unstable.)

"*When he brings Nicole and Alicia back after his time with them, do you talk then?*"

"*Sometimes, but only about the girls.*"

"*When he brings the girls back, do they look mistreated in any way?*"

"*Not on the outside, but they demonstrate negative things in their mannerisms.*"

"*What kind of negative things?*"

"*They stomp off to their room like they can't wait to get away from him.*"

"*Do you go to see why they are upset?*"

"*I have learned to let them cool down before we talk about their day.*"

"*When you have your talk, what do they share?*"

"*They are just glad to be back home.*"

"*So, they never say that they want to go live with their father?*"

"*No, never.*"

"*What if I were to tell you that both Nicole and Alicia have repeatedly cried when they left Jake and Terry's house, and begged them to not take them back to your house. Would that have explained why they stormed off to their room?*"

"*I would say that they were lying. They were always glad to be away from them.*"

"*That's interesting, Mrs. Wilson, that you would accuse them of lying. I have some letters in my possession that implies that you have lied to this court.*"

"Objection! We have not seen these letters," Joan's attorney blurted.
"Bring the letters to me and we will take a fifteen recess. I will leave to my chambers and be back to render whether they can be used in this case."

Judge Carter took the letters along with a short note as to their meaning. Joan and her lawyer hovered to discuss what the letters might contain. Joan appeared somewhat bewildered, as if she did not know their content. They were written over ten years earlier to Jake's stepbrother, while they were having a marital affair. She denied having that affair in the last custody hearing. Now Jake was hoping that her infidelity and lying would have a bearing on this case. There is something about telling a lie. Once you start, it is difficult not to tell another. The question was, could her latest testimony be more lies as a protection mechanism?

The minutes ticked away. Both parties seemed to be anxious as they waited for the judge's ruling on the letters. If this was a jury trial, the members would easily be swayed by the intensity and sexual innuendoes expressed in her words to Aaron. If the letters were made available at the previous hearing, Jake might well have won custody of his children, despite his record as an ex-con. Fifteen minutes seemed like eternity in that room.

"All rise," the bailiff announced.

Judge Carter took his seat at the bench and asked both lawyers to come forward. In a soft voice he gave them instructions about the use of the letters. Since he was the one to render the final verdict in the case, he let both parties know that he understood their implication. In the interest of time, however, he told Jake's lawyer to not use them any further in his cross-examination. Both men went back to discuss the matter with their clients.

Joan learned that the letters were written while she was married to Jake and discussed an affair with his stepbrother, Aaron. If looks could kill, hers would have slain an army. She could not believe that Aaron would even save the letters, let alone give them to his brother. Whether they would be captured by the court stenographer or not, they damaged her case.

Jake received the news from his attorney with a much different feeling. His lawyer assured him that the judge had read some of them and understood why they were being used at this time. The exuberance of his attorney's voice convinced him that a victory had been won. He may not win custody, but surely, any question about supervision would be thrown out. Jake smiled and Joan saw it. He could only imagine the angry feelings that roared inside her.

Joan was not asked to take the stand for further cross-examination. Jake's lawyer did not want her to make any attempt to counter the damage. He felt that Jake's witnesses offered a different point of view for the judge to consider.

JAKE'S STORY IS TOLD

It was now nearly three in the afternoon. The judge ordered a short recess before continuing the deliberations. Those in the back of the courtroom made a quick exit before Jake, who was still thinking about the events that just occurred. George Patterson stayed in the room, but nearly everyone else took the opportunity to refresh. George went up to Jake, put his arms around him and said that everything would be all right. His words were a great comfort.

> *"I just can't believe you are here, Harley. It's so good to see you again, not that I missed our sessions you understand."*
> *"You turned out just fine, Jake. I wish all my assignments were as good as you."*

Both men had a light chuckle.

Jake took his family down to the cafeteria in the courthouse for light refreshment. He did not notice that the judge was coming out of his chambers only a few steps behind them. Jake's interaction with his family was of special interest to Judge Carter. The picture painted by Joan's lawyer was in stark contrast to the one he was observing there. The children were laughing and had every appearance of loving their father, despite the fact that they were adopted. If he had earned their love and respect as their new dad, then how much more is the respect from his natural children? The thought so captivated the judge that he went back to ask the bailiff to locate Nicole and Alicia and bring them to his chamber.

> *"Jerry Hancock is the grandfather. Here is his phone number and address,"* Judge Carter instructed the bailiff.

"Have them here before five this afternoon," he insisted.
"Make sure that you bring them in through the back door to my chambers."

Terry sat across from Jake at a table, while their children enjoyed playing with some other kids in the cafeteria. They seemed to be communicating without words spoken. The events of that afternoon went better than either expected, but the rest of the day might prove otherwise. For that moment, however, they gazed into each other's eyes and smiled. Then Jake bowed his head and offered one more prayer for the rest of the session. They gathered the children and proceeded back into the courtroom. Jake's side of the story was about to be told.

As they entered the courtroom, Jake spotted another man from his past sitting in the back row.

"Johnny! Is that you?"
"In the flesh, Jake."
"But, but …what brings you here? You look like you cleaned up your act pretty well."
"Harley was called in to give the judge some personal information on how you turned out. Don't worry. I think he's on your side. He asked me to come."
"Yeah! I saw him earlier. At least neither of us have to report to him anymore, huh?" Both men laughed.
"Word has it that you have a plumbing business, a beautiful wife, and a new family. Sounds like a great life."
"You bet. Terry is the best thing that ever happened to me, aside from finding Jesus. Are you still reading that Bible I got you?"
"Every day, brother. Every day. Thanks to you."
"The judge is about to come in, Johnny. I better take my seat. Talk to you later, Okay?"
"You bet, Jake. We have a lot to talk about. It's been about eight years since we've had a good talk."

Both men took their seats and the judge walked in. Jake thought it was unusual that the bailiff had not announced his entry as he did twice before. Judge Carter sat down at the bench and addressed Jake's attorney.

"Are you ready to call you first witness?"

"I am, Your Honor. I call George Robinson."

George came up from behind Jake. As he passed, he grinned at Jake as if to say that everything would be all right. Jake smiled back in acknowledgement. After being sworn to tell the truth, George took the stand.

"State your name for the record, please."
"George Robinson."
"Why are you here?"
"I was asked to speak about Jake's character. I was his parole officer after he got out of prison."
"Who asked you?"
"Judge Carter."
"Now wait just one minute Mr. Robinson. I don't recall asking you to provide anything for this case," the judge remarked.
"Not you judge. Judge Carter was the man who incarcerated Jake. He asked me to come."
"Do you mean Judge Andrew Carter?"
"I do, but I never heard anyone ever call him anything but Judge Carter. Is he related to you?"

At that moment the judge leaned back in his chair and placed his glasses on the bench. He paused for a moment as if to take in the words that were just spoken. Andrew Carter was his father. This case was not on his docket until the last moment, and he had wondered why. He was supposed to hear a divorce settlement suit, but the original judge for the custody case asked if he would swap, due to a conflict. Both were considered civil cases, which required very little preparation, so he agreed. Knowing that his father orchestrated the switch took on new meaning.

The judge remembered his father talking years ago about a young man that he sentenced to four months in prison. His father took a special interest in the young man. There was something about him that warranted a watchful eye. Andrew Carter had a caring heart and enjoyed his work as a judge. Jake was very special to him. The judge gathered himself and picked up his glasses.

"Andrew Carter is my father. He must think your words are important or he would not have asked you to come. So tell me about Jake Wilson's character, Mr. Robinson."

"Thank you, Your Honor. First let me say that it is an honor to speak on Jake's behalf. He was assigned to my care as his parole officer after his release. If only all of my cases were as easy to manage as his."

"In what way, Mr. Robinson?"

"From the very beginning, Jake kept his nose clean, never missed an appointment, and was respectful. He enjoyed his freedom and it was obvious to me that he never wanted to set foot in that place again. The life he led prior to incarceration was over. He was determined to make a difference in society."

"Have you ever seen him angry or lose his temper, Mr. Robinson," the judge inquired.

"Not even once. He seemed to be at peace with himself. Often our sessions would be filled with more laughter than anything else."

"I take it, that you consider Jake is a good man, but what are your opinions as a father?"

"Jake had been married before. His first marriage ended in divorce, but it was doomed from the beginning. He slept with a married woman, while her husband was fighting across the ocean. They had a child together, a boy. Jake talked more about that son than anything related to his life; years after his sessions with me were officially over. We remained the best of friends. I truly believe that Jake would make a wonderful father."

While George Robinson was speaking about Jake's son, tears ran down his cheeks. Judge Carter was quick to notice that response. It was obvious that Jake was remorseful over his son and had the ability to show emotion. The man he was before entering prison's doors would never have shed a tear. Then the judge asked Joan's attorney if he had any questions of the witness.

"Thank you, Your Honor. Yes, I do have a few questions. Mr. Robinson. When was the last time you saw Jake prior to this case?"

"About six years ago. I was invited to their wedding and saw them casually in some local restaurants."

"So Mr. Robinson, how does that qualify you to testify about his character today. Don't you think people can change in six years?"

"All I know is that a good friend asked me to share and I want to honor that friend. As far as believing that people can change, of course I do."

"So then, is it possible that the man you knew, say six years ago, could be very different today."

"Of course it is."

"Do you think that raising children can change a man?"

"Yes. That's a tremendous responsibility."

"So it is possible that nurturing children could cause someone to lose their cool and even bring harm to a child."

"Yes, that's possible, even for a mother."

Up to that point, Joan could see where her attorney was going with the questioning. Suddenly, the direction seemed to backfire. Jake also seemed to smile at George's response.

"We're talking about Jake, Mr. Robinson. Is it possible that the man you knew six years ago could have changed? Can we believe whatever you tell us really applies to the present day?"

"That's not for me to decide. Judge Carter has to make that decision."

Judge Carter thanked George for his input and dismissed him from the stand.

"Call your next witness, counsel."

"I call John White to the stand."

Johnny came up from the back of the room. He was dressed in a nice suit and winked at Jake as he came forward. He took the stand after taking the oath.

"Please say your name for the court."

"John White."

"How do you know Jake?"

"We were sort of roommates together."
"And where was that?"
"The Florida Correction Institution."
"You mean prison?"
"That's correct."

Joan's attorney raised an objection.

"This man is a convicted felon. What possible testimony can he give in this case?
"Overruled," Judge Carter said emphatically. "Although I am wondering the same question, I want to hear what he was to say. Continue."
"When was the last time that you had contact with Jake, Mr. White?"
"It was at his wedding to Joan. I was an usher, and please call me Johnny." Jake smiled.
"So Johnny, that was a long time ago. Why are you here today?"
"While we were in prison, Jake had one visitor. In fact it was the only visitor either one of us had during our stay. It was Judge Carter, Judge Andrew Carter. When he sentenced Jake, he opened a Bible and shared scripture. Then he told Jake that he would make sure that he had a Bible with those words highlighted."

Judge Carter removed his glasses once again as if to keep them dry from the tear that slowly fell from his right eye. He grew up in his father's home and remembered the countless hours that his father would sit and read the Bible. It was because of his father's teaching that he desired to follow in his footsteps and become a judge.

"So, Johnny, did he deliver on his promise?"
"He did, Your Honor. He brought it personally. That meant so much for Jake. I think he had many people promise things in his past, but the judge followed through. They became great friends."
"That's it, Johnny? Is there anything else we should know?"
"There's far more. Because of Judge Carter and Jake, I was given an early release. The judge met with the warden and had

us placed in the same cell for a reason. He saw something in me as well." Another tear flowed down the judge's cheek.

"Continue Johnny," the judge insisted.

"We studied that Bible every night, often long after the lights were out. What I did not know until later was that Warden Jackson had several discussions with Jake's parents about becoming my guardians for the remainder of my sentence. That day, when I was told I would be released in their care was thrilling. I really missed Jake."

"So Jake's parents were pretty nice. How does that affect this case?"

"Oh! There's more." Jake leaned forward as if to make sure that he did not miss a word.

"After spending about two months with Jake and his family, they helped reunite me with my mother and I went to live with her. Jake totally changed my life"

"What do you mean?"

"I mean, because of Jake I am alive. I found Jesus and I owe it all to Jake. Those long Bible studies and our conversations led me to that commitment."

"So, Johnny. Do you believe that Jake is a changed man?"

"You bet. Neither of us can ever go back to the life we had prior to our prison experience."

"Do you think that Jake is a good father, Johnny?"

"Objection, hearsay," Joan's lawyer shouted.

"Overruled. I am interested in what Mr. White has to say," Judge Carter insisted.

"I think he would make a wonderful father. In fact, judging by what I have seen here today, I think he already is."

"Tell me Johnny, what are you doing with your life today?"

"I am a minister. I knew that I had a purpose and Jake helped me to find it."

Jake's jaw seemed to fall to the table below. It was the first time that he had heard of Johnny's intention to go into the ministry. He wanted to run up and embrace his friend, but kept himself in control. He recalled the hours and hours of discussing Ephesians 2:10 and what it meant. His life had taken the route of being a plumber, but he shares Jesus with every customer he meets. Johnny had taken a different route, but he was certain that God was looking down on them and smiling. Jake's heart was overjoyed at the news.

"Would you like to cross-examine counselor?"
"I have no questions of this witness."

The damage was irrevocable. Questioning a minister about issues regarding Jake's conduct as a father might further jeopardize their claim that he was prone to angry rages. Johnny was a very creditable witness. Just then, the bailiff returned to the room and whispered into Judge Carter's ear.

"Court will be in recess. Please stay here until I return," the judge announced.

While Judge Carter left the room, the bailiff remained to ensure order. Joan yelled several expletives that young children should not have heard. The wait was only minutes, but seemed like hours to both Jake and Joan. Then the doors opened.

"All rise," the bailiff announced.
"The Honorable Judge Carter presides," he continued.
"Please be seated."

Judge Carter scanned the audience for a brief moment and then began to speak.

"This has been an interesting case, but I think I can dismiss any more testimony. As I stated at the beginning, this case is about the welfare of two precious girls. I had them brought to my office and asked them a few questions. They are extremely bright young ladies." Judge Carter acted like he was clearing his throat.
"The first question I asked was, 'if you could chose which parent you would desire to live with, who would you chose?' They did not hesitate and in unison responded 'Daddy.' What was even more impressive was the joy on their faces as they shouted."
Jake had that same look of joy on his face as well.

> *"Then I asked them why they would rather live with their father. Each girl had a different answer. Nicole said that her daddy loved her, read stories and played games with her on those overnight stays. Alicia said that she was scared of her mother. I asked Alicia why she felt scared. She said that her mother yells a lot and hits her."*
>
> *"That's a lie,"* Joan screamed. *"I never hit her,"*
>
> *"The bruises that she showed me on her back and left thigh tell a different story. Now sit down before I have you arrested for child abuse."*

Joan's lawyer knew what was about to happen and tried to calm his client. Joan was out of control. The bailiff had to apply necessary force.

> *"It is the decision of this court that Nicole and Alicia be removed from their mother and placed in the care of their father until their eighteenth birthdays. Visitation rights by the mother will be determined by another court, but only supervised visitation will be the recommendation of this court, until Joan Wilson undergoes anger management and substance abuse tests. Only after such testing produces qualified recommendation, will this ruling be removed. Until and unless another court rules otherwise, this ruling will stand. Any child support payments to the mother will be terminated from this date forward. That is the decision of this court. Case closed."*

Jake leaped up from his seat and hugged Terry. It was not the decision he expected. Joan was a police officer. She always held the power in any confrontation. Judge Carter called Jake and his family to his chambers for some further remarks. As they entered the room, Nicole and Alicia pounced on their dad. It was a sight that spoke volumes about the decision being the right one. Jake and Terry had to sign a few papers to begin the finalization process.

> *"You will be hearing from my office in about two weeks. At that time you will come in to sign the official adoption papers. In the mean time enjoy your new family."*
>
> *"Thank you, Judge, thank you very much."* Jake said as he reached to shake Judge Carter's hand.

"No, Jake. Thank you," Judge Carter countered.

"What did I do, Judge?"

"You helped me see something that I had almost forgot, Jake."

"I still don't understand, sir."

"Andrew Carter was my father and mentor. He worked a lot, and I always thought I missed something while growing up. But, today I met a man who really never had a father until he met my dad. I think my dad had more children than I could imagine, and still I knew that he loved me. Sure, he came to some of my baseball games and other events while growing up, but I did not see him as often as I liked. It was because he genuinely cared about people like you. Now I see the fruits of that love. So, thank you, Mr. Wilson. Thank you very much."

"You could have ruled against Johnny's testimony, but you didn't. I just wanted to know why."

"My father changed your life, didn't he, Jake?"

"That he did, sir."

"You changed Johnny's. Don't you think that is something worth sharing?"

"I see your point, Your Honor."

"Now go. I see that you have two extra mouths to feed."

THE REFLECTION

Jake and his family left the judge's chambers through the courtroom. George (Harley) and Johnny were still in the room waiting to give their congratulations. For Jake it was like a reunion.

"Isn't God Great, Jake," Johnny shouted.

"That He is, Johnny. He's greater than anything I can dream of. If I am dreaming, please do not pinch me. I want to savor this moment."

"You're not dreaming, although maybe I am," Johnny replied.

"I wondered what you were going to say about me, Harley. You did good in there."

"I just spoke the truth. Didn't I hear somewhere, that the truth shall set you free?"

"I think that's in the Book of John, chapter 8, verse 32," Johnny responded. *"Jesus was talking to his disciples about knowing the truth. Jesus was the truth and you found him Jake."*

"You too, Johnny. What about you, Harley? Do you have a personal relationship with Jesus?"

"I believe in a Creator, Jake. I just don't know about why God would send His Son to die. It seems as though He could snap a finger and fix things. He has the power."

"How would you measure love, George?" Johnny asked.

"What do you mean, Johnny?"

"Do you have a family, George?"

"I have two boys. They are nearly ready for college now, so I guess they're not boys anymore."

"Do you love them?"

"Of course I do. What kind of a question is that?"

"Do you love them enough to die for them?"

"If that was a choice that I had to make, then I would die for them."

"Jesus tells us that there is no greater love then to lay down your life for another. Read John chapter fifteen and verse thirteen. That is what Christ did for us, George," Johnny continued.

"But, I don't understand why Jesus had to die. I don't consider my life in any danger."

"That's precisely why, He had to die. Your life, Jake's and mine are all in danger."

"Danger from what, Johnny? Who is trying to kill us?"

"The devil is, Harley," Jake inserted.

"This is getting really weird now, guys. Now Satan is in the picture."

"Satan has always been in the picture, as far as this world is concerned. He used to be an angel, but when he rebelled against God, he was sent to call the earth his home. God could have ended his life, but loved him enough to spare him. Satan has dominion over this world, but this world is not our eternal home."

"You mean heaven?"

"I mean eternal bliss my friend. This world is sure filled with a lot of things that we might not consider safe, enjoyable, or peaceful," Johnny added.

"If heaven is such a perfect place, then why did God place us here?" George continued.

"Now that's the sixty-four thousand dollar question, George. Have you ever wondered why we have the ability to seek God, while all other creation does not?"

"I haven't given that any thought, but that indicates that we have a special connection."

"The very first chapter of the Bible tells us that we were created in His image. A committee in heaven handed down that decision. Verse twenty-six of the first chapter of Genesis says, 'Let us make man in our image.' We were singled out as a very special part of God's Creation. Later in the book of Genesis you

will read that God breathed into man and only man. Yeah! I'd say we were special." Johnny continued.

As Jake listened to Johnny share the Gospel with Harley, he was amazed at how far his friend had come from those late nights in the prison cell. Johnny's knowledge of scripture had surely grown. Jake had attempted to read the Bible through, but always seemed to fall short in completing the task. He took his family out to the well-lighted atrium, while the others continued their discussion. He could see that Johnny was driven to have one more soul registered for heaven. He instructed Terry to wait until the men came out of the courtroom.

About ten or fifteen minutes later, George and Johnny came out. Jake recognized the look on Harley's face as the same one that Aaron had the day that he told Jake he had accepted Jesus in his heart.

> *"So George, do you understand the mystery?"* Jake said with a joyous smile on his face.
> *"I think I got it, Jake, but I have more work to do."*
> *"You have the rest of your life, Harley."*
> *"I know Jake. I also have a family to share with."*
> *"Do that, George,"* Johnny added *"and don't be ashamed of your decision tonight."*
> *"Hey guys,"* Jake interrupted. *"Remember the tattoo that I had?"*
> *"Its hard to forget a ball-and-chain with your inmate number, Jake."*
> *"It's gone my friends. I had it removed and replaced a week or so ago."*

Jake had his friends move towards a large window where the light was the brightest and pulled up his trousers. At the site of the old tattoo was a new one with three crosses. Jake refused to wear shorts for a long time after his conversion, as the tattoo was a vivid reminder of who he used to be and not who he is now. He wanted the world to know that he was a child of God. He was not ashamed of it.

> *"I never liked tattoos, Jake, but that one is amazing."* George said with a warm smile.

"It sure is better than the old one," Johnny added.
"I thought so too guys, and I work a lot in shorts now. That's a blessing in itself. People look at it without the same measure of disdain that they had with the old one. When I had the ball-and-chain, I felt powerful. It screamed, 'Don't mess with me.' Somehow I feel even more empowered with the new one."
"Here we are, Jake. We all have our crosses to bear, but we can do it together. We are brothers in Christ." Johnny added.

After the men departed, Jake stood on the courtyard steps for a moment of reflection. His earthly father abandoned him as a child. Now he was reunited with his heavenly father. He felt invincible as a teenager with a piece under his belt, but always expected someone to attack. Now he was at peace. Aaron spared him from a beating as a young man. Now Aaron was sharing the same peace of God as a believer. Today, Jake leaves the courthouse with his family complete. The only regret in his life still unsettled is his son. Perhaps, God will close that chapter as well.

Note from the author

Jake is a real person, though not his real name. I met him through a friend, who asked me to write his story. Although my story has a conclusion, his life is still a wonderful work in progress. Many of the events in this book are true, especially as they relate to his early adult years. Today, Jake is a devout family man with a genuine love of God. His story inspired me and I hope it inspires you.

Dennis can be reached via email at
(dennismcintyre6@gmail.com)
and welcomes responses from readers.